GRIM HARVEST
AN APOKÁLYPSIS NOVEL

Rachael Atkins

This is a work of fiction. Names, characters, places, and incidents are either the product of the author's imagination or are used fictitiously. Any resemblance to actual persons, living or dead, events, or locales is entirely coincidental.

Copyright © 2023 by Rachael Atkins

All rights reserved. No part of this book may be reproduced or used in any manner without written permission of the copyright owner except for the use of quotations in a book review.

First paperback edition October 2023

Book design by Rachael Atkins
Edited by Paul Atkins

ISBN 9798864063606
ISBN 9798864265703

Published by Amazon
www.ratkinswrites.wixsite.com

For Lily

Publish and Be Damned

PROLOGUE

In the artificially frosty air of her bungalow, an elderly woman bent over her kitchen sink. Among the coffee-flecked cups of last month and plates besmirched with next Tuesday's dinner, swirled the glittering vapours of the Infinite Void – a map of every 'was', 'is', and 'will be' in the known universe. It also makes very effective degreaser.

'Oh, buttocks!' the old woman shouted and banged her fists down on the metal draining board with a clang that sent ripples through centuries of time and space. Some of the mystic liquid hiccupped out of the washing-up bowl and splattered over her pink sandals.

'Double buttocks!!'

It is so very, very hard to wash Destiny out of suede.

The woman frowned and wrinkled her nose as murky figures, dancing in the Void, played out their little lives in front of her. She ran her bejewelled, gnarled hands through her candyfloss hair and shuffled over to her phone.

Minutes ticked by as she waited for the other end to pick up with a faint click, thousands of lifetimes away.

'Lennie, it's Sybil. I need a favour.'

CHAPTER ONE

A DEAD END

Max's scrambled brain was attempting to piece her whereabouts together like a woodlouse presented with a sheet of algebra.

A dull ringing in Max's ears gave way to the sound of Dolly Parton cutting through the thick stew of her thoughts. Her eyes remained shut – perhaps this would all turn out to be a dream if she refused to visually process this present reality.

Working nine to five...

'Car stereo. Why can I hear a car stereo?'

Her chest felt tight and she wondered if she might be having a panic attack. Her fumbling hand touched the smooth, cold seat belt pulled taut around her torso.

You dream about it, don't you?

'Seat belt. A belt...for your...seat'

Max felt the metal clasp wedged against the seat's upholstery and pushed down on the release button. It wasn't clicking. She pushed again and again.

Crazy if you let it...

'Cars have seat belts.'
'Car.'

Max opened her eyes and realised too late she was upside-down in the wreckage of her car.

Click!

She barely had time to let out a sharp shriek of surprise as she dropped out of the seat and fell head first onto the glass-strewn roof below her. The little shards tinkled all around as curls of grey dust linked arms and waltzed in the air.

She had managed to expertly wedge the entire front half of the car deep into a thick hedgerow just outside the village of Chudleigh – a place so sleepy as to be almost unconscious. The car interior was in complete darkness. She gingerly clawed her way out of what was once her beloved Ford as Dolly's dulcet tones faded from her ears, batting away blindly at treacherous brambles and nettles.

The night air was cold and still as she finally emerged into the moonlight, yelling indignantly, and stood up. In the near distance she could see the light from a house. Somebody was just discernible standing at the window, peering out. Hands on hips.

'Nothing to see here,' Max said under her breath, pulling a thorn out of her shaggy, black hair and noticing her hands shaking. 'No, you carry on watching the show, matey. Have a rant online about millennials and their driving abilities! Don't come and help me or anything!'

She moved forwards and felt a crunch underfoot – a piece of wing mirror. Parts of her car were strewn an inexplicable distance from the wreck; a door handle here, a page from the owner's manual there. A pine tree air freshener with an unnaturally happy face was blowing on the wind as if hoping to return to the origins of its forest scent.

An hysterical laugh escaped from Max's mouth. Her lips felt numb.

Following the lines of burnt rubber down the road and into the various black shapes hinting at the countryside beyond, Max began to recall the journey. She had finished a tedious night shift at the supermarket. The long evening had been filled with perfectly aligning cereal boxes. Eight hours all accompanied by the omnipresent squeak of trolley wheels on polished vinyl and the ghostly faces of night shift workers in search of a quick microwave meal.

Heading out into the night with a bag of stale bread rolls and a profound longing for quiet darkness, Max had trundled homeward in her beaten-up car. She yawned cavernously as the white lines of the road flashed underneath her one by one.

A rat, diligently washing his ears, was suddenly struck by a compulsion to cross the road. Max came racing down the lane and spotted a brown flash dart from right to left. Instinctively she had swerved to avoid it.

While she had saved the life of the young rodent, swerving to avoid anything at forty miles per hour is generally assumed to be a bad move.

She surveyed her wrecked vehicle with some sadness - its insurance was due to renew in a month. Her mum was going to kill her.

She turned resolutely to flick two fingers at the rat now darting back and forth along the verge.

'You don't even know what an insurance premium is!' she shouted at him.

She didn't think it was possible for animals to look guilty, but if it was, this was the guiltiest looking rat that ever lived. Twitching his little nose, he thanked his preferred deity and finally found a break in the hedgerow to escape through. For the rest of his natural life he would tell tales of the day he faced off against a Ford Anglia and won.

Max patted down her pockets and realised with a groan that her phone was still in the car. For a half second she considered crawling back in, but one look at the half-buried licence plate poking out of the branches changed her mind.

'Right then,' she said, turning back to the illuminated house. 'Talking to strangers it is then.'

With that, she began marching up the road towards the imposing gates.

Meanwhile, somewhere just south of Junction Twenty-Five, a being not dissimilar in appearance to a man, was driving his pale green campervan on the only road into Chudleigh.

An hour previously, Graham Reaper had been attempting to shepherd a particularly chatty lady in Birmingham to a waiting ferry. In fact, just five minutes ago he had been shouting at a man on Ben Nevis that his untied shoelace didn't matter anymore. Now Graham was in the middle of losing his temper. Something usually suffered whenever he did that.

Today was a Monday and Graham's patience was always thinnest on Mondays. So is most people's, but luckily not everyone has the power to inadvertently maim with a single thought.

Many creatures had borne the brunt of Graham's impatience in recent years. His beloved campervan now had a persistent ant infestation because Graham had forgotten his PIN number one too many times and completely lost his cool at an ATM in Tottenham. An entire neighbourhood colony was suddenly struck down with a debilitating migraine as a result. They had sought Graham out and taken up residence in the van's recesses, plotting to block the exhaust pipe when it was least expected.

It was now a fixture of Graham's Wednesday evenings to delicately open the boot and lob in several currant buns to placate the horde. They often screamed back with some of the foulest language ants can possibly muster when their mandibles are jammed up with icing.

Graham was quietly sizzling as the campervan approached the village boundary.

Max had made it up the driveway by now – shrouded in darkness by the surrounding trees. The light from the house's living room was her only guide. She knocked hard on the door and waited for some signs of life, but nobody came. She decided to open the letterbox.

'Hello?' she shouted. 'Look, I'm really sorry, I know it's late, but could you help me? I think you saw me? I had a bit of a prang. I hate to be a bother, but I think I'm in shock. I've probably got a hairline fracture somewhere. Super embarrassing. I just need a phone.'

Only silence followed. Max walked into the pool of light created by the living room window and peered in, jumping back in fright at the sight of a man in his sixties asleep in an armchair. She rolled her eyes and hesitated uncomfortably for a second. She knocked on the glass and just for a second she was sure she saw the curtains twitch.

'Um, sir? I'm really sorry... please wake up!'

Just then, a new sound was becoming audible in the distance – the rumble of a car drawing near. Over the hedgerow, dazzling headlights broke over the tallest branches. A sense of relief began soothing Max's shredded nerves like chamomile to a burn.

The headlights came around the corner as the car drove through the gate and rumbled up the driveway. Max turned to squint into the full beams, flapping her arm in the sky in the universal gesture for: 'You're blinding me, you berk!'

The van slowed its approach, and ground to a halt a few metres ahead, gravel shifting under its tyres.

Max had anticipated the driver would step out to assist, but nothing happened. There was only the sound of the wind blowing through the fields and the occasional hooting of an owl. If she could speak owl, she would've understood the bird's stark warning, but then this would be a much shorter story.

Max and the van were now in a standoff on the driveway. She scuffed the ground with her shoe.

'I'll come to you then, shall I?' she said and began marching back down the drive and into the triangular light of the headlamps. 'Unbelievable.'

As Max got closer she realised the van was painted a shade of green so unusual it made one instantly uncomfortable. She gestured to the driver to wind his window down.

'Would you mind giving me a hand here?' she asked.

A great, long, exasperated sigh echoed from inside the car's pitch-black interior. The sounds of fingers drumming on a leather steering wheel were clearly audible. The aforementioned owl fell silent, gagging on a recently caught field mouse.

'You're dead,' Graham growled from inside the darkness.

Max started running and didn't stop until she reached the gates to the house, illuminated by the light of the moon.

She peered behind for any signs of pursuit. She had heard of road rage before, of course. There was a story in the local paper recently about two men nearly killing each other with travel kettles after a minor prang just outside Chipping Norton.

There was the sound of limping footsteps and coughing. Graham emerged from the darkness of the drive.

Max had a better view of her pursuer now. He looked alarmingly like the guy at the convenience store on her road – thin, unkempt hair and sloped shoulders. He was wearing a beaten-up bomber jacket over a sweater of some kind, jeans and trainers. He had the air of a person who hadn't slept in roughly five million years. Because he hadn't.

'You made me run,' he said, wheezing as he followed her.

'Listen, creep,' she shouted. 'Back off, alright? Get away from me, right now.'

'Let's not do this, eh Max?' Graham said, motioning back and forth between the two of them. 'You're actually dead. You died. I'm going to have to take care of you.'

'Argh! How do you know my name?' Max said. Scrabbling to get out of the situation, she found all her sentences at once. 'There's no need for threats. You were just sat there in your van, not really apparently helping, which is super weird by the way, and I needed help and I just wanted to go home. I don't even have a travel kettle. Please don't kill me.'

Graham rolled his eyes - eternity was feeling particularly long tonight.

CHAPTER TWO

A SCYTHE OF RELIEF

'Where are we going?' Max asked as Graham's van whizzed left at a junction so fast it felt as though it had bent light beams.

'I told you – the ferry,' he said as a muscle in his eyelid twitched. He glanced over at his passenger, her fingers throttling the seat belt so hard they had turned white.

'Relax,' he said. 'You can't die twice.'

This did little to relieve Max. She was in no mood to have two car crashes in one night.

She felt her fingernails beginning to hurt: 'Do you have to drive like a maniac?'

'Actually, yes.' Graham said, pushing his foot down hard on the accelerator with no effect for the umpteenth time. 'I usually have a lot more horsepower. Something's upsetting my loyal steed here. You've not got anything heavy on you have you? Magnetic? Radioactive? Salty?'

'Ooh! Let me think,' Max said, relinquishing her death grip on the belt just long enough to pretend to pat down her own pockets. 'No, I must have left my plutonium pretzels in my other dead body. Why?'

With no warning, Graham swerved sharply into a layby.

'Hop out a second,' he said.

'You're a lunatic,' Max said. 'You can't just take people hostage like this. I'll call the police!'

Graham leaned across Max and opened the passenger door.

'If you please,' he said and gestured for Max to get out.

She stumbled out and began running up the roadside. She heard the campervan engine revving behind her and turned to see it pulling away. No sooner had it built up some speed, the front seemed to stretch forwards in a heartbeat like an elastic band before the back eventually snapped to catch up. The entire vehicle blinked out of sight. Max stood dumbfounded.

'I shouldn't have eaten those bread rolls,' she said. 'I can't be dead. Can I? This isn't happening.'

The air was cold and crisp. High above Max's head she heard a flock of birds pass by. Their squawks echoed over the valley beyond.

Max could feel emotions rushing into the void in her brain that Graham had inhabited from the moment his van had appeared on that dark driveway. Pins and needles rippled across her body. They bounced off her fingers and swirled around her waist, down her legs and pinged off her toes. The life she had left behind so suddenly flashed in her mind; her mum, her job, her bed – sitting still unmade in the darkness of her room. There was a more dominant feeling though, above the grief.

'What is that?' she asked the hedge. 'I'm not sad. I'm not anxious.'

Before the hot tears had chance to tumble down her cheeks there was a mechanical screeching and the campervan reappeared from around the bend in the road pulling back into the layby.

Max felt her teeth grinding on each other.

'I'm angry!' she said with a sudden sense of realisation.

'You see?' Graham said, winding down the window and calling out to her. 'It's definitely you. I just reaped a thousand souls right there. It's going to take hours to get you to the port, pest.'

'I'm really dead?' Max asked. The tingling feeling was fading fast.

'I'm afraid so,' Graham replied sarcastically. 'I'd ask you to tell me all about what happened, but I don't really care. Now get in.'

'Charming. I'm so glad the blow of this traumatic time is being cushioned by a kind and caring companion.'

There was a brief silence as Max climbed into the front passenger seat once more.

'Do I call you Death then?' she asked.

Graham cleared his throat as he started the engine: 'You may call me Graham.'

Before Max could reply, a muffled ringing noise in Graham's coat pocket interrupted her.

'Aren't you going to answer that?' Max asked.

'I already know who it is,' Graham replied. 'They'll have to wait. I need a drink.'

Steam fogged up the café windows so that only humanoid, blurry, multi-coloured blobs seemed to be passing by outside. Occasionally one looked up from the glowing rectangle it was holding and sneezed.

The fluorescent lighting flickered off the glasses of the waitress as she presented plates of food to waiting tables as if she were dolling out helpings of arsenic. There were seven framed portraits of her on the walls, each with a plaque reading 'Employee of the Year'.

'You're not what I pictured at all,' Max said, sitting opposite Graham at a small table by the window.

'Yes,' Graham said, only half listening. Most of his attention was being spent lustily inspecting the large hot chocolate in front of him, piled high with cream and marshmallows. 'I suppose you were expecting the big robe? The black? The scythe?'

'In a nutshell.'

'We decided to move away from all that. Turns out nobody really knows what a scythe is these days. The symbolism works wonders for the agricultural community, but for everyone else, not so much.'

'I feel sick,' Max said. She turned to the window and cupped her face in her hands to check it was still with her.

Graham glanced at her indifferently before attempting to make eye contact with the waitress. He needed more sugar to add to the six cubes he had already dropped into his drink. His phone buzzed on the table.

'This jacket,' Max said, 'I can feel it. How can I be dead if I can feel? I got it for Christmas last year.'

'Such a shame for you,' said Graham, taking a big sip of his drink and grinning.

'Right? A stranger tells you you've kicked the bucket and then bundles you into his van.'

'It really is awful.'

'This is what I'm saying!'

'You couldn't return it or anything?'

'Return it? Oh, the coat. Very funny. How can you be so cold about all this? You're talking to a dead woman in a café in…where are we?'

'Somewhere in Dorset,' Graham gestured vaguely in the air with his spindly fingers.

'You're sipping your coffee and quipping away about my choice of clothing.'

Graham asked for the sugar again as the waitress bustled past for the third time. 'I have to find some ways to amuse myself.'

His phone lit up with a more insistent buzz. He turned it over and closed his eyes, attempting to search the dark annals of his mind for a scrap of calm contentment. A flock of pigeons on the café roof held their breath.

'Are you listening?' Max asked. 'This is my big moment, my end of days! I'm sat here in yesterday's underwear and you couldn't give a flying pig!'

'It's a 'flying fig',' Graham said.

'What?'

'The phrase is 'I couldn't give a flying fig'. Like a flying f-'

'No, it's pig, because flying pigs don't exist – just like your ability to care.'

'Well, I can't argue with that logic.'

The waitress shuffled past and slid a cup of sugar into Graham's waiting hands and an egg on toast to Max.

Max's eyes narrowed: 'You ordered me egg? I hate eggs.'

'Well, don't eat it then!'

'Where's the solemnity? The dignity? The golden staircase, harps and cherubs? I want my 'pearly-gated-choral-singing-respectful-dudes-in-white-gowns' moment!'

'Enough!' Graham said through his teeth, slamming his fist on the table. 'I'm Death, you tiny, insignificant moron! Psychopomp, reaper of souls, one of the four horsemen. Ringing any bells for you?'

Nobody in the room seemed to bat an eye, but the pigeons on the roof simultaneously developed crippling diarrhoea. Max could've sworn the café grew a little darker and Graham a little taller as his eyes burned fiercely.

'Your manners are atrocious!' she replied.

'Here's the thing, Max,' Graham said more calmly, which was almost worse than the spitting. 'You're not special. There's no grand plan. You're just one soul in a very large queue for the exit and I'm the guy who's about to boot you out the door.'

He reached inside his coat pocket and pulled out a palm-sized device resembling a tablet.

'Look,' he said, turning it on and waiting impatiently as it flashed into life. He dragged his finger clumsily across the screen. 'Where is the...? No, I don't want to update my system. I just want the list. No cookies! No! Hold on, hold on.'

Max steepled her fingers and stared down her nose as Graham hunched over the glowing screen.

'I hate this thing,' he said. 'Right, right! Here you are! Yadda, yadda, yadda... died today at 12.45am, Chudleigh.'

Max tried to get a look at the screen.

'No peeking,' he said as he scrolled down the list of names. 'This is all the other people who have joined you in death in the last hour.'

'Well, why even bother with the café then, if this is such a 'wham, bam, thank you ma'am' kinda deal?' Max asked.

'This isn't for you, you narcissist,' Graham replied. 'I can't function without a sugar hit!'

'Not a very deathly drink is it?'

'Yeah, well death's too long not to treat yourself. Consider this little pit stop a blow softener.' He slung back another mouthful of whipped cream and marshmallows. 'A rare easing, if you will, into the hereafter.'

Max looked around at the other diners: 'Are all this lot dead too?'

Graham shook his head slowly.

'Then why aren't they fussed about our whole situation here?'

Graham leaned in close to Max as he swallowed: 'They're alive, but I didn't say they were human.'

He straightened up again as Max looked half horrified, half curious at the perfectly average looking group of people eating their breakfasts all around her.

'Now, we've got a ferry to catch,' he said suddenly. 'So I'd appreciate if you could finish not eating so we can get a move on.'

With that, Graham produced a crumpled bank note from his pocket and dropped it on the table. Max was still processing everything. It had been a very trying morning. She stared at the money.

'That's a pound note.'

'Yes, very generous I think.'

'I saw one of those in a museum once. You know we stopped using those in the olden days, right?'

'No wonder I get such terrible service in here.'

Graham reached further into his pocket and this time pulled out a fifty-pound note and set that down instead as Max looked on in shock.

'That should buy me some good grace. And the Eighties are not 'olden days', kid. I've been around since the BCs! Now it's time to go.'

Max looked bleakly at her untouched egg and toast and it stared back at her in much the same fashion. Its edges curled up as if it were reaching out for a hug.

'I guess that's the end of it,' she said to the egg. 'I never thought I'd die young.'

'Well' Graham said, swiping the egg with a fork and swallowing it whole as his phone buzzed again. 'Your time is up, everything happens for a reason, you're in a better place et cetera, et cetera.'

'Whatever,' Max said. 'Just dump me where you're planning on dumping me. You're lucky I'm taking all of this so well. I'm dead, I should be absolutely beside myself.'

'Under the circumstances you probably were for a minute.'

'More jokes from Death? Marvellous. Hiding your trauma through comedy by any chance? How's your relationship with your mother?'

'Maybe you're not upset because there's nothing to mourn,' Graham said.

'Excuse me?' Max rose from her chair and stared at Graham with an intensity he was not accustomed to.

'Bet it was a boring, sad, little life,' Graham shrugged. 'Your troubles are over now.'

Max continued staring at him. One thousand cutting remarks raced through her brain, but she remained silent as she pushed her chair in with a screech and a slam.

'I wish I wasn't dead!' she shouted, marching out of the café door with such vigour she nearly broke the handle.

The waitress shuffled over to grab the plates and rolled her eyes at a shell-shocked Graham. 'Kids, eh?' she laughed.

CHAPTER THREE

CORPORATE MANSLAUGHTER

The campervan squealed to a halt outside a petrol station. Max took a deep breath as she once again unhooked her fingers from the seat belt.

Graham yanked up the van handbrake like he was calling a hellhound to heel and opened the passenger door.

'I could go faster with a sled pulled by sloths,' he huffed. 'Out, out, out!'

He wafted the air in front of the door as if a breeze alone would displace Max. She watched her breath spiral upwards in the cold air and pondered whether she was choosing to exhale to preserve her sanity or because she still required oxygen.

'You're going to need to wait here while I go and deal with some souls who don't slow my van down,' Graham said.

'Suits me!'

'Settle down there, squirt. I'm not leaving you on your own.'

'Please, I'm not a baby. You can pootle off and do your... stuff.'

'Yeah, that's a hard no. You need a guide to keep you tethered. Without one you'll just drift off, like a... like a helium balloon.'

'Sounds delightful.'

'You'll be lost entirely. Every wisp of remaining consciousness stolen from you and the chance to live on in The Afterward gone forever.'

'Oh,' Max said, her smile fading rapidly. 'I'll take the guide, please.'

Graham nodded smugly as he rifled in his pockets for his ancient phone. It looked like it was held together with sticky tape and blind faith. He dialled a number.

She spotted a bus stop across the road and sat down on the sheltered bench underneath it. There was the sound of flapping in the sky and Max looked up to see several hundred black birds flying together like a swarm. It made her feel comforted, though she couldn't understand why.

'Yes, Azrael...yes I'm aware you've been calling,' Graham blared, one hand leaning on the van door. 'I know that! ... Look... look...look! I don't know why it's happening, van's having a funny five centuries. I know I'm falling behind. Can you send Doris, please? Azrael... Azrael... Az... that's not helpful... can you just send... send the bird... please... thank you.'

Graham joined Max at the bus stop.

'I spy with my little eye, something beginning with D,' Max said with a smirk.

Graham gave her a withering look: 'Don't be ridiculous.'

'No, guess again.'

'Do shut up?'

'No.'

'Damn, I hate my job?'

'Play properly, come on! And then, if I win, I get my life back, right?'

'Impressive Bergman reference, but no, that is very much not how this works.'

Max rolled her eyes: 'It's death. That's the answer. Death!'

'I should have got that, ' Graham said. He nudged Max in the ribs and pointed to a small, black smudge in the sky. 'Say hello to your babysitter.'

Max stared as the smudge grew bigger. It was another black bird. It descended gracefully and landed with the minimum of flap on the ground in front of them. Its glossy wings shone in the sun and its eyes were gleaming and curious.

'When you said bird, I assumed you were being derogatory,' said Max.

'Alright Doris?' Graham asked and Max nearly yelped in surprise when the bird replied with a noise that sounded an awful lot like 'harrumph'.

'Watch this one for me, will you?' Graham asked. 'I'll be back shortly!' He leapt in the van and winked out of sight in a furious rush.

'I feel like I have many questions,' Max said quietly.

'I sensed that,' Doris rasped with a voice like a witch with laryngitis.

'You *can* talk!' Max said, eyes widening. 'You're a talking crow?'

'Raven, if you don't mind.'

'Sorry. And you babysit dead people?'

'Broadly speaking, yes, that is what ravens do. Babysitting is a bit of a reductive term. Although, I thought I was personally past all that now – moving up the corporate ladder, you know? I'm Azrael's secretary these days.'

'Azrael is...?

'The Angel of Death.'

'I see,' Max said as if it were the most normal thing in the world. 'So why are you here with me and not writing memos for the damned?'

'Because Mr Reaper still treats me like a paperweight for ghosts and my boss likes me to keep an eye on him.'

'Sorry.'

'No bother. You seem like a nice one to be minding.'

'You seem like a nice raven.'

'Very kind of you to say.'

From the distance there was an almighty mechanical scream and the campervan whizzed back into view on the quiet, country road.

Graham leaned out of the driver window and shouted at them: 'Having a good natter, are we? Let's get out of here! Doris, you're coming with us in case I need this one minded again.'

Before Doris could protest, Graham's phone began ringing. For the second time today, Azrael was calling.

'What is it now?' Graham snapped. He pushed the van door open and marched towards the nearby petrol station.

'Stay in the van,' he shouted as Max and Doris looked at each other.

'Can you get me a sausage roll?' Max replied, but Graham was already halfway up the station forecourt.

He ripped open the door and pounded down the snack aisle with the phone jammed to his ear.

'Oh, Graham, what are you up to?' Azrael said, her voice tinny and crackling in the phone speaker. 'Why are you taking so long today?'

'Do you know, Azrael,' Graham hissed through gritted teeth, 'we've sometimes gone whole centuries without speaking?'

'Yes, Graham and wasn't that just glorious for all concerned? But things are beginning to slow down a bit today. Dangerously so.'

'Perhaps, and I don't mean to reinvent the wheel here, if you stopped calling me I could get on with the job?'

'Clever, but I think it's actually your pace that's the issue here.'

'I told you. The van's having some trouble, Azrael,' Graham said. He could feel the tension building in his jaw – tightening the gap between his top and bottom teeth until not even atoms could pass through. Every bird and beast in a two-mile radius was on tenterhooks.

'Fill in the Transport Complaint Form when you're next in the office,' Azrael said, 'in triplicate, remember and co-signed by the mechanic and we'll get you a replacement within five working centuries. It's really very simple.'

Graham hated conversations with middle management. Always sticking its celestial fingers into his dead pies. Always fussing about with the divine and meddling in the mystic. His methods had worked for the last five million years, so why change anything? But, no, in came the targets, the metrics, the charts. Oh, the charts!

'You'll have to prise my van from my cold, dead fingers,' Graham said.

'Your fingers are literally cold and dead.'

'Yes, so?'

'Well, when someone alive says that... it doesn't matter. Anyway, that soul in Chudleigh – you've not dropped them off yet. Any reason for that?'

By the time he reached the crisp section Graham was breathing so heavily he sounded more like an express train. He picked up a bag of popcorn.

'I really just felt it was worth us touching base,' Azrael said, sensing the aggravation in the silence. She tucked her bobbed hair behind an ear and tapped her foot nervously from the safety of her office, hundreds of miles away. 'You've had a bit of an anger management problem for a while, Graham. And mistakes are being made. I'm sure I don't have to tell you we can't afford slip-ups in this line of work.'

Graham moved to the chilled meats, picked up a pork pie and began squishing it inside his fist until the meat oozed out of the plastic wrapper.

'I'm not angry, Azrael.'

He glanced sideways at the checkout, shook the pork off his hand and carried on perusing.

'Explain all the wildlife that keeps on mysteriously suffering in your company then. Don't think we haven't noticed all the ducks with gout, pony migraines, and snail shingles!'

'I've been doing this job for a long time, Azrael,' Graham said. 'The longest, in fact, so I'd appreciate some faith.'

'Not to mention all the poor souls you've been mucking about,' Azrael said as she uncurled a piece of paper from her breast pocket and began reading from it. 'Three months ago, you left the soul of one Mrs Ethel Saxby in your car for two hours unattended.'

'I needed a milkshake! I wound the window down.'

'Yes, but she climbed out, didn't she, and fell down a manhole.'

'I found her eventually,' Graham retorted as he moved to the checkout and put the bag of popcorn on the counter in front of the cashier and another fifty pound note.

'Just in time, more like. Two weeks ago, at the ferry port you were heard telling Mr Guy Potmonger, and I quote: 'Good riddance, you pervert.''

'He did strange things with houseplants!'

The cashier looked at Graham with alarm. He inspected the note too quickly, handed back the bag and change and decided the stock in the backroom had to be checked immediately.

Azrael said: 'Since when do we make judgements on the dead?'

'Actually, some cultures would tell you that's exactly what I do,' Graham replied.

'How convenient for you. And now today everything's hit the brakes. You're well behind schedule. It's been hours some people have been waiting. You know how critical it is that we make a good first impression.'

Graham had stopped listening, the phone in his hand hanging limply at his side as he inspected the rows of magazines.

'Hello? Hello Graham?'

'Oh, you're breaking up,' Graham said half-heartedly.

'Oh whatever! Just be careful, Graham,' Azrael said. 'I'm afraid if this pattern continues you're going to make a mistake you're really going to regret.'

'Ooh,' Graham muttered sarcastically. 'Don't tempt fate, Azrael.'

'Right, goodbye then,' Azrael said curtly as she hung up.

'Thanksgoodbye,' Graham said as he marched out of the petrol station, popcorn under one arm.

He waited a full two seconds before he allowed himself a small yell of indignation. He could feel a headache coming and went to pinch the bridge of his nose. Too late, he remembered the pork still clinging to his fingers.

CHAPTER FOUR

DEATH IN DENIAL

The ferry port was a seething ants' nest of exhaust-spouting machines driving onto slightly larger exhaust-spouting machines. It had started to rain and the streetlights reflected off the water, decorating every bleak surface with a jarring spray of sparkle.

The campervan snaked its way past queue after queue. Men and women in high visibility vests waved their arms as if hoping to tie them in bows. Traffic lights shifted colour lazily as ferries opened their mouths wide and swallowed cars whole.

'So which ferry does one board to begin eternity?' Max asked sleepily, Doris perched on her shoulder.

'Actually none of them,' Graham replied. 'We've missed the 6pm boat, so you're going to have to stop here for a bit.'

'What?' Doris and Max squawked in unison.

'Can't we just magic up another boat?' Max asked.

'No,' said Graham. 'For the fourth time today, this is not magic. There was an age when a single ferryman could sail back and forth at will and take one soul at a time, but now there are just too many for a little rowing boat, so we fill up two ships' worth every day at 6am and 6pm.'

'Two ships for the whole world? Seems pretty stingy.'

'You humans,' Graham rolled his eyes. 'Always thinking so three-dimensionally.'

'Are you saying it's bigger on the inside?'

'No, I'm saying just because it looks a certain size and shape, doesn't mean it is.'

Max looked very confused.

'You think the sky is blue, but it isn't – it's just the way all the cones and rods in your eyes process what you're seeing.'

'Urgh, you sound like my old Philosophy teacher. So deep, do tell me more!'

'Well, he sounds like a very smart man!'

Max rolled her eyes: 'Spare me!'

The van turned a corner and entered a quieter part of the port.

'What'll it be then? B&B?' Max yawned. 'Warehouse? Toilet block? I wouldn't be surprised at this point.'

But the van carried on, past dry docks and sleeping forklifts and chain-link gates until it reached a derelict office block, far away from the bustle of the main dock.

'Blimey,' Max said, fidgeting in her seat. 'If I weren't already dead I'd be worried you were about to murder me.'

'Keep pestering me and I'll try and find a way! This is your home for the night, madam. Welcome to the Easy Slumber.'

Graham gestured with a sarcastic flourish, as if it were the top prize on a TV game show.

From the outside, the hotel did not look like a natural fit for a restful night's sleep - a brutal concrete cube, dirty with age and riven with cracks. Its windows were boarded up and there was no sign of life within. Spikes on every ledge kept even the bravest of birds from roosting. Doris shuddered at the sight of it.

'Easy Slumber,' Max said, staring up at the aggressively ugly building. 'Sounds like a funeral home.'

The trio approached the grimy door and Graham grasped a worn, wooden handle and pushed. They stepped inside, finding themselves in an equally grim and almost completely dark antechamber, no more than three metres square.

'Well,' Max said, 'I don't know why I expected anything different. Sweet dreams!'

But as Graham pushed open a secondary door, the vestibule flooded with golden light and Max found herself agog for the first time since her death.

Beyond the second doorway was the unmistakable sight of a hotel lobby. The polished wood floors reflected the glittering chandelier above them, sending fractured splinters of gold across the room. Red velvet curtains hung from every window but they displayed nothing but planks of wood and black paint. Most breathtaking of all was a grand staircase, gilded with gold and adorned with cherubs, which stretched out in front of them,.

'There's your golden staircase,' Graham said in reaction to Max's open mouth.

'As in *the* golden staircase?'

'Mr Reaper!' A man dressed in a bus boy's uniform had spotted Graham and was beckoning him over.

'Did you hear that?' Graham said, beaming. "Mr Reaper'. I love this place.'

He strode over to the desk as Max went to explore the lobby with Doris.

'Not bad,' Max whispered, brushing a hand over a curtain as she passed and feeling its soft, flocked texture.

'Just because you're dead, doesn't mean you can't live the high life!' Doris said.

All around were what Max assumed to be various fellow souls – some old, some young, some very young. Some looked as if death had been a relief and others as if it had taken everything. Some were on their own, some in groups, some in crowds. Every one of them seemed to be accompanied by a raven. The more she looked, the more Max realised it seemed more like a five-star detention centre than a hotel.

'Fancy, isn't it?' Graham said, suddenly appearing out of nowhere and sending Max hopping in the air in fright. 'I got you a suite!'

As they walked down the third-floor corridor, Max noticed that each room had a slightly different door - a varying shade of cream, a sticker or two, crayon marks half cleaned away, a tiny ornament hanging from a handle.

'We're just up here,' Graham said as they turned a corner, only to be greeted by another long corridor filled with doors.

Even before she had reached her room, Max knew she had arrived. The door was so familiar she felt a pang in her heart – the bedroom door she had opened, closed, slammed and ripped open in excitement from her childhood until the day she left for work for the last time. Her height was marked up the frame every year until she was thirteen. She had grown too embarrassed then and refused to let her mum measure her anymore. Graham passed her the key and she recognised it at once - right down to the smear of pink nail varnish she had placed on it to tell it apart from the back door key.
She hardly dared put it in the lock, but something drew her in.

'I'll be right outside,' Doris said reassuringly, flying from Max's arm to Graham's shoulder.

Everything was as Max had left it. The flower-speckled duvet sat crumpled on top of the bed. The multitude of colourful books gathering dust on her bookshelf. Her favourite perfume bottle perched on her bedside table, lid lying next to it.

Max had barely stopped to think about anything resembling normal since her accident all those hours ago, but now her senses were overwhelmed and she felt the strongest sense of loss smack her full in the heart. She felt a pain in her chest for herself, for all the things she would never do, all the friends she would never make, and the places she would never go. This was really happening, she was really gone.

Max felt herself getting very short of air. She bolted for the door and flung it open. Graham and Doris were waiting in the hotel hall.

'It's too much. I can't sleep here!' she said.

'I had a feeling you might say that,' Doris said. 'Some people find it a comfort. Some, like the people you saw in the lobby, do not.'

'Then why have the option?' Max shivered.

'Well, a lot of people who die suddenly seem to like it – the chance to say goodbye. It brings them comfort. Plus, there's not a hotel room in the world more comfortable than your own. But it's not real, you know – just a copy.'

Max hesitated on the threshold, pondering Doris's words.

'One sec,' she said and disappeared back into the room.

She stood in the silence and took a deep breath. She felt the pile of the plush pink carpet shift under her feet as she gazed out of the window. The street was quiet today. She checked the bedside clock. Any minute now, Nancy from next door would be getting home from work, wrestling with whatever weird and wonderful charity-shop discovery she had stumbled upon during her lunch break and stashed in the boot of her car. Mr Martin across the road always walked his dog at this time – sure enough Max heard the sound of footsteps approaching quickly as he was dragged around the bend by Flossy the Great Dane. Max giggled at the sight of him, in spite of herself.

She ran her hand slowly over the floral duvet, dropped the room key and picked up a paperweight on her bedside table. It was a gift from her mum, a daisy flower suspended in glass, perfectly preserved for the rest of time. Before she could take a closer look, it slipped from her grasp and landed with a resonant thud on the floor.

Somewhere in the distance below her, Max heard a chair scraping on the kitchen floor. A woman's voice said faintly: 'Hello?' It was her mum.

'Mum? Mum it's me!' Max replied, her voice breaking.

Footsteps were running quickly up the staircase on the other side of the door and the voice was louder now. 'Hello? Who's there?'

She sounded tired and frightened.

Max wiped away a tear and rushed to open the door only to find herself stood in the hotel corridor staring only at a very confused Graham and Doris. She whipped around to go back into the bedroom, but the door had already clicked shut behind her.

She shook the door handle over and over but it was no use.

'I lost the key inside,' Max sobbed. 'My mum's in there!'

'Have you lost your mind? I thought you didn't want to spend the night in there,' Graham said.

'That's not possible, love,' Doris said flapping onto Max's shoulder and placing a comforting wing on her head.

'I think I can recognise my own mother's voice!' Max said. 'I put the key down to pick up a paperweight. But I dropped it and my mum heard the noise and then I ran to open the door to see her and I was back out here.'

'No, you must be confused,' Graham said. 'You shouldn't have been able to hear your mother. It's not really your bedroom, you see – it's just a facsimile, like I said. You must have made a mistake.'

He stared intensely into Max's frightened eyes and said slowly: 'It's not real.'

'No, I heard her say hello. I have to get back in there!'

'Listen,' Graham said, fixing a smile as the cogs in his head turned. 'It's been a long day, you're still in shock.'

'What are you talking about? I heard my mum.'

Doris looked at Graham: 'This doesn't sound right.'

'It can't have been your mum, Max,' Graham said, fixing a smile as the cogs in his head turned. 'The only way you could have possibly heard her is if you still had a strong connection to the living world which is highly unlikely because you are extremely dead."

'But I heard footsteps on the stairs?'

'In fact, the only possible way you could have heard your mother is if you were still alive!'

'Well then –' Doris said.

'You're tired, Max,' Graham said, avoiding Doris's gaze. 'Let's go down to the lobby and you can kip on a sofa. Still alive? Ha!'

CHAPTER FIVE

THE TERMINAL TERMINAL

The next morning, Max jumped into the now familiar front seat of the campervan. In the dark sky above, she could hear an almost constant sound of beating wings.

'All those birds. There must be a lot of souls waiting for you,' Max said to Graham as she leaned her head out of the window and stared up, seeing nothing but the black sky. Graham was focused on the street ahead, lost in thought.

'Hmm?' he said. 'Did you say something?'

'What is up with you this morning?' Max swivelled to face Graham. 'You were like this at breakfast – you barely touched your crumpets. Graham? Graham?'

He was lost again, wrestling with a sense of uncertainty he had only just discovered in the last twenty-four hours.

'Come on then,' Doris bristled as she flapped in through the open window, snapping Graham out of his internal monologue. 'Let's go to oblivion - if that's what you want!'

The van made its way past the queues of waiting cars, lorries, mopeds, and motorbikes, all vibrating with the anticipation of travelling on the wobbliest of all forms of transportation.

Under the streetlights, Max could see baffling road markings which wound their way over and around each other as if dancing a ballet. Sea salt clung to the wind and lashed every building, vehicle and face that it could find.

As they drove up the road, the walls of the surrounding buildings seemed to push in on them. It felt narrow and claustrophobic. Max peered out of the window and it slowly dawned on her with a dreadful weight in her stomach that they were, in fact, now travelling in the shadow of a monstrously large ship. Its inky black hull rose up like a skyscraper. It seemed to absorb all light around it - almost as if the entire vessel was merely a silhouette. Max didn't want to look at it, but she could not tear her eyes away either. It made every bone in her body itch.

Graham turned to Max and smiled: 'I know it looks bad, but there's actually an on-board cinema and a surprisingly entertaining yoga class, so...'

'There's no way I'm getting on that thing,' Max whispered.

'Millions of people do it every day! What's the worst that could happen?'

Max saw a gangway sloping down from a door in the side of the ship. A line of foot passengers snaked up it and disappeared inside. Graham had been out all night attempting to catch up on the many thousands of souls twiddling their thumbs for salvation.

'You could just leave me with that lot,' Max said gesturing to the queue.

'Yes, but you've been a particularly prickly thorn in my paw,' Graham said. 'I want to make sure you're dealt with.'

'Oh sure,' Doris said. 'Nothing to do with any misgivings, eh Mr Pefect?'

'Keep out of it, sticky beak!'

The van cleared the stern of the ship. The road turned towards another, much larger gangway leading to a huge steel door at the ship's rear. Trucks, vans, cars, and several mopeds were queuing to embark. Graham pulled the van in to back of the line.

Max turned round, snapped out of her morbid fascination with the ship: 'What did Doris say?'

Doris opened her beak to reply, but before she could answer Graham swerved suddenly out of the queue.

'What was I thinking?' he said. Doris looked hopeful for an instant, before he continued: 'I'm Death, I don't queue!'

He cut in at the front of the line, much to the chagrin of the other drivers. An officious woman with a clipboard motioned for Graham to wind down his window before she could utter a word.

'Checking in, sir? You do realise this is the staff entrance?' she said bobbing her head about like an owl to get a better look at Max.

'I hardly think those technicalities are necessary for the Graham Reaper, Miss…?' Graham said, searching for the woman's nametag.

'Of course not, sir! I do apologise! What was the name?' said the clipboard woman as she pointed to the nametag on her lapel in answer to Graham's question.

'Thank you… Ethel. Ethel? Lovely. It's Max Mallory.' Graham shot a glance at Max, but she was talking in hushed tones to Doris with a look on her face that worried Graham greatly.

A commotion of some kind was audibly building somewhere in the back of the queue. A vehicle was revving its engine.

Ethel went up and down her list with a pen. Finally she said: 'Ah yes, here we are. Uhh, no wait this can't be right. Two seconds.'

Graham glanced in the rear view mirror. The engine was revving very loudly now.

'I'm sorry, what did you say?' asked Graham, raising his voice above the cacophony.

The din behind them grew louder still. Suddenly, a blue moped came barrelling through the lines of traffic at great speed and zipped past Graham's van. Max could just make out a tiny rider dressed in a black leather coat and motorcycle helmet with a shock of pink hair peeking out from under it. She could've sworn they were screaming 'Tallyho!' over the sound of the engine.

'You best get on that,' Graham said to Ethel before she hared off after the speeding bike now streaking into the bowels of the ship.

'Well,' said Max. 'On any other day, I would've said that was a bit weird.'

'Yes,' said Doris, flapping onto Graham's shoulder and digging her sharp claws into him. 'And very convenient,' she whispered.

'High time you flapped off back to Azrael, isn't it, Doris?' Graham asked.

'Can't you come with me?' Max said. 'You're nicer than him.'

'I'm afraid not, actually,' Doris said. 'I can't travel to The Afterward because I'm alive and I belong in the mortal realm. The crossing could kill me. Right, Graham?'

She nipped Graham's ear with her sharp beak and made him cry out.

'Bye then, Doris!'

'I hope we meet again one day, Max,' Doris said, hopping over to her. 'Remember, what I said? Please keep your ears open.' Then she jumped to the open window and flew off into the distance.

Graham pinched the bridge of his nose in exasperation, then restarted the van and drove over the ramp and into the ship. His stomach was in knots. What had Ethel been about to say?

'Well this is...groovy,' Max said, hand on her hip and utterly perplexed, as she and Graham stood on the ship's main concourse.

Every surface of the ship's interior seemed to be one shade of brown, orange or a combination of the two. There was carpet on the floor and, in an effort to double down, even more carpet on the walls. Everything was vaguely tinged with a smell of cigarettes and aftershave.

'Well, now we know where the Seventies came to die,' Max sniffed, as they walked slowly through the room.

'Yep, well it's where you've come to die too,' Graham said. 'The ship leaves in five minutes.'

His phone was ringing again. After all his good work last night he knew he was falling monstrously behind on the reaping.

'So what now?' Max asked. 'I play shuffleboard and do the nightly bingo until we reach The Afterward?'

'You'll make the crossing, yes.'

'And then what?'

'Well, that's it. The Other Side.'

'Yeah, but then what?'

'Well, you're just sort of done, aren't you? Game over.'

Max looked at Graham with an air of suspicion: 'You don't know, do you?'

'What do you mean?' Graham said uncomfortably.

'All this time and you've no idea what it's all for!'

The pair stepped abruptly into a massive, brightly-lit atrium - some nine-storeys high and lined with shops, bars and cafés. They were all making preparations to open for the voyage across the ocean to The Afterward. People were mingling too, peering in windows and talking quietly to each other.

Interestingly, there's a shopping centre somewhere in the vicinity of Kettering, which bears a striking resemblance to the lobby. The architect had a near-death experience around 1983 and spent a few short minutes on board the ferry before he was rescued and sent back home. He remembered very little of the whole affair, but from then on, his work featured angular glass roofs and a pervasive sense of the inevitability of death.

A woman dressed in varying hues of black thrust a balloon into Max's hand. 'Enjoy your voyage,' she grinned. 'No photos, please!'

Max smiled back weakly as the woman bounced off to another unsuspecting gaggle of passengers. Max stared at the balloon. On it, in faint chalky letters, were the words: 'Die, Laugh, Love.'

At the centre of the atrium sat a giant marble fountain spewing black water. A small, skeletal automaton in a wooden rowing boat was paddling in circles across the water.

'That's Charon – the ferry man,' Max said, pointing at it, as Graham's mouth fell open. 'Don't look quite so shocked! I love Greek mythology.'

From high above, they heard the sound of approaching, galumphing footsteps followed by an almighty bellow.

'GRA'M? IT *IS* YE!'

Graham slapped his forehead: 'Speak of the devil!'

Max looked up just quick enough to spy a towering figure place a hand on the glass balustrade of the fifth floor and vault over the top. She let out a scream and stumbled backwards as he hurtled down at tremendous speed and smashed feet first onto the floor in front of them, completely unscathed. Graham did not move a muscle.

'You always did know how to make an entrance,' Graham said flatly, eyes rolling.

'GOD MAN, IT'S BEEN MILLENNIA,' Charon said as the dust settled. He clapped Graham on the back so hard he nearly flung him into the fountain.

'Why is he still shouting?' Max whispered.

'He's a shouter,' Graham replied, adjusting himself after the slap. 'That's just what he does.'

'WHA'S THE SPECIAL OKAYSHUN THEN, LAD?' Charon said in a piratical accent veering towards parody. He adjusted the cap on his head as he scratched at the shaggy grey hair underneath and pulled a crawfish out of it. 'YOU DON'T NORM'LY DO PERS'NOL ESCORTS!'

'Well, I thought it was high time I checked in on your whole operation,' Graham said shiftily. 'Make sure everything's running smoothly.'

'What happened to seeing off "your most prickly of thorns"?' Max said.

'It can be both!' Graham replied too quickly.

Charon turned to Max and bent forward to see her better, his green eyes darting across her face from one micro expression to the next: 'AN' WHO MIGHT YE BE, MISSY?'

Graham butted in just as Max began to take a breath: 'Just a soul – an average, run-of-the-mill soul of no importance.'

'YOU SEEM AWFUL YOUNG. ACCIDENT WAZZIT?' Charon asked, looking her up and down.

'Do we really have time for pleasantries?' Graham said. 'I'm on a very tight schedule!'

'It was a car crash,' Max answered. 'I lost control and woke up in a hedge.'

Graham's face fell: 'But you were at the house?'

'Yeah, I saw a light on and walked over to the cottage for a phone. Guess I didn't realise I was dead!'

'You didn't tell me that,' Graham said affronted.

Max folded her arms and stared back at him: 'You told me you didn't care about the details, remember?'

'LET ME SEE,' Charon said, producing a ship's manifest from his pocket. 'AH, GOT A BROTHER IN GLASGOW, SO'S I HAVE!'

Max smiled politely: 'Okay. Good for you, I guess?'

'WHERE IN THE CITY WERE YOU BORN?'

'I wasn't. Do I sound like a Glaswegian?'

'EH?'

'Alright, this has been special. Shall we go now? Maybe grab a hot chocolate?' Graham asked quickly, grabbing Max by the shoulders and attempting to direct her away. The sinking feeling in his stomach could sink no lower. His worst fear was now realised with terrifying clarity.

'GRAHAM REAPER!' Charon said with petrifying volume. 'LET HER GO!'

Graham's hands dropped limply to his sides as Charon turned to Max and showed her the manifest. 'I THINK YOU BETTER HAD TAKE A CLOSER LOOK AT THIS, MY LOVE.'

She scanned each line as Graham chewed his nails. Charon shot him a glare as cold as the Atlantic as they waited in silence.

'Graham!' Max's head lifted up from her reading.

'Hmm, what?' he replied, with a fake air of nonchalance.

'This isn't me!'

She stared straight into Graham's flickering blue eyes for perhaps the first time since they had met. For one brief and terrible moment the entirety of time and space flashed in his fathomless pupils. Icicles of fear seemed to stab at Max's chest.

Time slowed for a moment before Graham let out a long, low groan. He put his hands over his eyes: 'Could you not pretend to be...' he paused to read the words on the form through his fingers, 'Max Mallory? Civil Engineer? Sixty-five? From Glasgow? It'll be fun.'

'Uh, no? I'm Max Godwin, supermarket stock management assistant, thirty, from Dorset.'

From deep within the bowels of the ship, a low vibration began moving through every floor until it shivered up the pillars of the great atrium and made the potted plants jiggle.

'ARE YOU'M TELLING ME YOU'VE REAPED THE WRONG SOUL?' Charon said in some distress.

'Keep your voice down!' Graham said.

Max flapped her hands like a grounded crow - her mind spiralling as she paced back and forth.

'Listen,' Graham said, half to himself. 'I'm sure you're really dead, there's just been a mix up with the names somehow. Or you just died at the same time as this other Max and he or she is waiting at the cottage. Two people can die simultaneously, it happens all the time.'

Max started pacing back and forth as the vibration settled into a gentle hum.

'Do you actually hear yourself?' she asked. 'No, I'm not. I'm not dead, I know I'm not.'

'That's just not possible,' Graham said, but his words had lost all their authority.

'All of this could have been avoided if you'd bothered to ask me one thing about my life or looked at your damn tablet for more than a nanosecond!' Max raged. 'You suspected, didn't you? When I heard my mum yesterday in the hotel room. You fobbed me off and told me I was tired, but I knew I wasn't! The van doesn't work with me in it either! Doris warned me, but I figured you'd pipe up if you really believed something had gone wrong!'

She shook her head as she came to a startling realisation: 'You would have let me cross over, wouldn't you? The Grim Reaper was perfectly happy to bump me off to save his own fragile ego! ... I... I have to get off this boat.'

Max's mind became a blur of thoughts and she ran blindly out of the atrium and down a corridor.

'YOU'VE TORN IT NOW, SONNY,' Charon said as the floor beneath them began to vibrate. 'THA'S THE ENGINE STARTIN'. WE'LL BE SAILING ANY MOMENT. YOU BEST GET HER OFF THIS RUST BUCKET, WHOEVER SHE IS, OR SHE MAY NEVER GET BACK ALIVE.'

Graham took off down the hallway after Max. He was not what you would call a natural runner. Pipe cleaner limbs moved through the air as if leaping up invisible stairs. Doors passed by in a flash and the patterned carpet became nothing more than a long streak of orangey brown - corridor after corridor, down stairway after stairway. Finally, he rounded an unremarkable corner and nearly took flight as he tripped over his own feet and landed at Max's crumpled form on the floor.

'There you are,' he said breathlessly as he straightened himself and adjusted his sweater.

Max's head remained bent low, resting on her curled up knees. She sniffed: 'I couldn't go any further, this ship is a labyrinth.'

Graham sat down next to her, grimacing as his knees cracked.

'You're right,' he said. 'I haven't been taking things seriously enough.'

'You've been jumping to conclusions about me from the moment we met. You never asked me anything. I was just a name on your stupid list. Not even the right name, as it turns out!'

'Okay, you've got two options – you cash in your chips, stay on this boat and properly die. Or we go back and try to untangle this little mystery. It'll be a lot of bother and a massive inconvenience, but I'll do it if it'll put your mind at ease.'

Graham stared at Max's face as she considered her situation.

'Stay?' Graham said rising to his feet. 'Good choice, nice and tidy. A lot easier for me. It's been fun. Have a nice afterlife.'

'No, no, wait. I'm not ready to go! I want to go back. Of course I want to go back.'

'Argh, really?'

'Yes!'

'Are you absolutely sure, though?'

'What do you mean?'

'Well, life's not all that great, is it? Taxes? Cleaning toilets? Stubbing your toe? Mondays?'

'The other stuff makes it worth it though. More than worth it. The lie-ins, trees, buttered toast, holidays, Christmas, bubble baths… and my mum.'

A lump caught in her throat: 'My poor, lovely mum.'

'Take it from me, kid. You're just going to end up working, sleeping and then dying. You might eat some nice food, you might see some pretty places, but that's about it.'

'You really are disillusioned with your job, aren't you?'

'Eh?'

'You just don't get how wonderful life is. If you did, you'd have a bit more respect for people who had lost theirs. I've always feared you. Feared going young, going at all. But I don't fear you now. I pity you, Graham Reaper.'

'Oh, how's the oxygen up there on your moral high ground? I get everyone in the end from serial killers to soup kitchen volunteers. I'd tell people to make the most of what they have, but by the time I meet them, it's too late. None of it matters!'

'It matters to them!'

'Let's say you're right and, by some miracle, you're really not supposed to be here. Have you made the most of your life, Max? Something tells me not.'

'What right have you got to lecture me about living my best life?' Max said. 'You're so bored of your own existence! You haven't been making the most of death, how's about that? I'll tell you something else - you're going to get me off this barge and put things right.'

'We might be too late already,' Graham said, pointing out of the window in front of them at the port shrinking off into the distance.

By the time Max and Graham made it to the ship's deck, the port was just a smudge on the horizon.

'Oh no,' Max said hopelessly. She was beginning to feel very unwell.

'There must be some way we can still get you out of here,' Graham said. 'I don't suppose the ship to The Afterward carries lifeboats?'

'Surely you have checks in place to stop this sort of thing happening?' Max said.

'You'd think so, wouldn't you?' Graham replied, the salt wind licking his face like an old dog. 'Do you know over 150,000 people die around the world every day? That's 104 every minute. And I've been doing this for five million years.'

'So how did you end up reaping the wrong soul, Mr Experience? I suppose that's my fault, is it?'

'I mean, yes, quite frankly. Why didn't you just stay put with your car? Someone would have found you eventually.'

'I needed a phone to call for help! You said the other Max was in that house you found me next to? I think I saw him, you know. Maybe he's still there wondering what the deal is. If your system thinks you picked him up already then nobody's looking for him.'

Graham yanked his coat collar up. 'I'm still not convinced.'

He pulled out his tablet and began flicking through the names.

'What did you say your surname was?'

'Godwin.'

'G, g, g...' he traced his finger down a collection of surnames, up and down over and over again.

'I'm not there, am I?' Max said. A wave of light-headedness passed over her again and she felt her fingers wrap around the edge of the bench for support.

'Maybe the system has somehow overwritten your name in the confusion?' Graham said doubtfully. He couldn't even convince himself.

'I'm not dead, Graham.'

He looked Max in the eyes and the two of them shared a moment of understanding new to both of them. It was a baffling experience for Graham, who was so emotionally impoverished that any sense of connection with a being of any kind felt itchy and alien. Just for a second he believed Max completely – overwhelmed by the mountain of evidence and the absolute conviction in her eyes.

'I was meant for more,' Max said emphatically. 'I was only 30 years old and one singular rat crossing a road polished me off!'

They returned to sitting in silence with only the sound of the crashing waves for company. The sky was darkening and the sea was slowly turning to a velvety purple. The crosshatched pattern of waves spread out as the fathomless abyss of waters eternally flowing between worlds carried them onwards. The Afterward was approaching. Max wasn't sure how much of her was still alive, but she had the sense now that something was leaving her, she was shedding layers like falling leaves on a tree.

'Wait,' Graham started. 'Did you say rat?'

'Yes,' Max rolled her eyes as she inspected her own hands, half expecting them to have turned translucent. 'Don't laugh.'

'You're sure?'

'Yes, I'm sure. It was massive. I swore at it when I got out of the car...when I thought I got out of the car.'

In a dimly-lit corner of Graham's mind he felt the beginnings of a spark of suspicion. A fraction of the big picture was coming into focus. For the first time in two days he knew what he had to do next and the feeling wrapped itself warmly around him.

CHAPTER SIX

FRESH MEAT

Beep!
Beep!
...

Beep!

'Oh, naff off!' screamed a duvet piled up on a bed like whipped cream.

An impeccably manicured hand stretched out of the cosy cocoon and batted the phone off the nightstand where it continued to whine, face down in the carpet.

The duvet rippled and out of the chrysalis emerged Azrael. She groaned as daggers of sunshine pierced the pitch-black bedroom and needled her eyeballs.

'Monday,' she strained as she brushed the hair from her face and slid out of bed, finally attending to the phone that was still having a muffled screaming fit in the shag pile.

She scanned the long string of messages. It seemed she wasn't the only one on a go-slow this morning.

'I'm going to need lots and lots of coffee.'

When patients are admitted to Restdown General Hospital, somewhere in the vicinity of Swindon, they often remark to Todd the porter how strange it is that the lift skips the thirteenth floor. Todd dutifully replies that the entire building skips the thirteenth floor as the number is believed to be bad luck. This, bizarrely, makes total sense to all enquirers, but Todd is a minion of the apocalypse and Todd is lying.

On the floor between 12 and 14 sits the headquarters for the four horsemen, recently consolidated under the umbrella corporation Apoco Ltd.

Every morning, the staff of several hundred minions trudge the 26 flights of stairs to their office. One by one they file into the white, wipe-down nightmare that is Floor 13 where the walls seem to huddle together for safety and everything smells dully of antibacterial floor cleaner and Parma Violets. All the staff that is, except the archangels and members of the board, who have the privilege of using the executive elevator.

Thanks to some mildly illegal bending of reality, Floor 13 boasts a squash court, vineyard, and an exact replica of the bar at The Ritz Paris. Executives had been known to spend years in there, emerging after thirteen storeys and two decades with an acute knowledge of Merlot and a bad case of tennis elbow.

Today, the executive elevator doors parted with a particularly impatient PING. Azrael squeezed through the gap before the doors had fully opened, then galloped down the corridor – her trainers squeaking on the vinyl floor.

She burst through the doors of her office - her phone was flashing so frequently with updates, it looked like a strobe light in her pocket.

'You okay, Azrael?' asked Doris, who was knitting a sweater at her desk, the needles clutched between her talons.

Azrael rounded on her. 'Doris, you know I love your cardigans, but I don't pay you to cable stitch.'

Doris gulped.

'I pay you to help me with this!'

Azrael twitched, bending over and wiggling Doris's mouse. The computer was brought back to life and revealed a tidal wave of messages.

'Ooh blimey,' the bird said, placing her knitting to the side. 'So sorry, I must have had the volume down.'

'Get on it, please,' Azrael sighed. 'Then set up a call with Graham, thank you.'

'Okay.'

'And for the love of all things holy, fetch me a cappuccino... please!'

The late morning sun draped itself across the office carpet as Azrael hung up on her call to a garage forecourt in deepest darkest Devon.

'Right, off you pop then,' she said as she took off her headset, flopped down in her chair and began banging her head against her desk.

Doris flapped in and settled on top of the in tray as Azrael stopped and sat motionless with her face down.

'Everything okay?'

'I need a favour,' Azrael began and the bird sighed. 'Listen, I'm sorry, but our mutual friend has requested you help him out and it would really help *me* out if you helped *him* out, okay?'

'Oh Azrael,' Doris said, folding her wings indignantly. 'I thought we were past all this?'

'Just this once, Doris. Please? It's just a small babysitting job in Devon.'

'There's no such thing as a small job. You know that.'

Azrael enviously waved the bird off through the open window.

'You owe me one,' the bird shouted before the archangel returned to her desk, imagining the crisp pure air of the countryside.

The cacophony of panicked noises emitting from every electronic device in the office slowly quietened to a light dirge as the day wore on. Like white noise, it became almost soothing. Every raven at Azrael's disposal was out sitting with the waiting dead, but she finished her shift knowing there was still little hope of catching up.

Crawling back into her car, Azrael began to dare to hope to imagine that she may very soon be back in bed. She allowed herself the tiniest sigh of relief as she started the long journey home to a waiting ready meal and her favourite box set. A sigh she would live to regret.

'HE'S ON THE WHAT?' she screamed from the office floor the next morning, desperately focusing on the polystyrene ceiling tiles to avert an incoming panic attack.

Doris was perched above the door, her head in her wings.

'HE'S ON THE FERRY?'

'I'm afraid so!'

Azrael rolled her eyes:"Take a job as Death's archangel,' my father said. "People are always dying,' he said. "Nothing is certain but death and taxes!" But Death's not certain, is he? In fact, he's incredibly unreliable! He's having some kind of mid-death crisis and I'm picking up the pieces!'

Doris' computer made an ominous noise. It was less of a beep this time and more of a chime.

'For whom the bell tolls,' Azrael wailed as Doris flew to check the message.

'It's an emergency board meeting. They want you in there right away.'

'I'll bet they do. I'm doomed.'

The boardroom was as cold and sterile as a surgeon's knife and just as sharp in places. Shadowy figures sat around a long rectangular table - a sea of square shoulders and squarer minds. All, that is, except for a small figure at the back, unremarkable in appearance, save for the smallest hint of a pink curl of hair.

'Send her in,' one of them muttered and from behind a pair of double doors strode Azrael. She had replaced her comfortable trainers with a pair of black high heels in an attempt to channel her inner warrior. Her toes were begging for forgiveness. Nothing but a slight shake in her knees betrayed her inner fears.

'Good morning,' she said as the doors closed behind her. She stood at the head of the table. 'How are we all today?'

The shadowy figures had no mouths as such - more a rippling void of undulating black mist. Nevertheless it soon became apparent that one of them was speaking, addressing her with a voice like an unspooling cassette tape: 'Did you have an update on the Reaper situation?'

'Yes,' Azrael nodded, her voice quivering. 'So it appears... he got on the ferry.'

She had anticipated immediate anger, but the room remained as still as a cathedral.

'Alone?' one of the voices asked.

'No, with a soul who may or may not be dead.'

'Is this soul on the list?' a shadow added.

'There is a Max on the list, but possibly not the right one...'

'What does it matter if it's the right one? He's got a soul with him who's clearly dead. On the ferry they go!'

'Well,' Azrael swallowed, 'I'd say there's perhaps enough evidence...'

'Perhaps?' a shadow scoffed. 'Reaper's time management skills are abysmal. We do not have the capacity for him to be holding hands with souls like this.'

'It's time wasting, Azrael,' another added.

'Time we don't have,' a shadow from the back chimed in.

'Our entire operation is falling apart,' another disembodied voice said. 'We have a queue of souls backing up that will take weeks to clear.

'When is he coming back? Is he coming back at all?' another voice asked.

'I don't know,' Azrael replied, feeling a bead of sweat trickle down her back. 'I'm working hard to manage the situation.'

'Not hard enough, Azrael. I'm afraid we've had to make arrangements in Reaper's absence. He's clearly checked out, burned out, or maybe he's just time he was out for good. Who knows?'

'I admit he's been a bit off lately,' Azrael said. 'He seems angry, stressed, maybe even bored. He's gone an awful long while without annual leave, you know?'

'How long?'

'Maybe four mega-annums? Does he even have a holiday allowance?'

'Our most pressing problem is to start getting souls reaped before the world is overrun. Ghost sightings have quadrupled.'

One shadowy suit produced a phone, tapped the screen a few times and held it aloft.

A video with neon subtitles and winking emojis appeared showing a woman apparently doing the Macarena with her dead nana.

'Obviously, that's less than ideal,' Azrael coughed. 'But rest assured, I'm thinking out of the box to expedite a solution.'

'The wheels are already in motion, Azrael. Send out the ravens to guard the souls already waiting...'

'I have.'

'And Simon will take care of the dead shortly.'

One of the shadows pointed extravagantly towards the boardroom door. Azrael did not care for the theatrics one little bit. The door creaked open and in stepped a hulking meat triangle of a man. He was more than six-foot tall, stuffed into a suit approximately three sizes too small, and had appeared to have forgotten his socks.

'Who in the blue blazes is this?' Azrael gestured as Simon sidled up to her and flapped his arms slightly as if he'd meant to wave and thought better of it.

'We have, let's say, manufactured a replacement for Graham. We call him Simon Coe-Pomp.'

Azrael couldn't help wincing. 'Manufactured?' she asked.

'Yes!' one of the voices chuckled. 'We had a little joke going that a chicken could do a better job, so we dressed one up a bit and here we are.'

'He'll be more reliable, faster, and more efficient than Graham ever was,' another voice added. 'Frankly, we've been itching to replace him for years.'

'Howdy,' Simon beamed, flashing teeth so white they could function as searchlights.

'Simon here is going to revolutionise the death industry,' a shadow said.

Simon was still smiling, the corners of his mouth twitching with the strain. His head bobbed slightly back and forward.

'Right then,' Simon said suddenly, clapping his hands loudly. 'Let's get a team briefing going, Azrael. We need communication moving upwards, downwards and sideways.'

Azrael blinked: 'Excuse me?'

Simon continued: 'I'll need a cup of corn and a glass of tap water and then let's go reap some souls, yeah? Top stuff.'

He strutted out of the room, his knees hardly bending as if incarcerated in their tight trouser prison. Azrael wasn't sure what to do next so she did a little curtsy to the board members and then ran after Simon. Somehow she beat him to the office. Doris was busily packing a bag.

'Doris, you're back! Thank goodness!,' Azrael whispered. 'Listen, there's a chicken called Simon coming. He's Graham's replacement. You have to get out of here for me.'

Doris' beak hung open for just a second as she processed what she'd just heard. 'I'm hoping if I rearrange those words something resembling sense will appear, but I'm sure I heard the word "chicken" mentioned, so possibly not.'

'I don't know how I can be any clearer.'

'But I've been called up,' Doris said. 'I have to go babysit some other damn soul somewhere.'

'No, no, no,' Azrael spoke quicker and quicker, hearing Simon approaching. 'I want you to go to Chudleigh. Investigate Max Mallory's house for me. Something isn't right here and I trust your instincts. There has to be a clue there somewhere. Quickly, go now, please!"

She ran to the office window and opened it wide as Doris struggled to understand.

'Out out out!' she said and gently ushered the protesting Doris out of the window for the second time in two days.

'Charming!' Doris muttered as she shook her feathers out and flapped towards the horizon.

Azrael swung round as Simon sauntered in and clucked involuntarily.

'Great idea,' he said. 'Get that window open and let in the fresh air. I like the free range feel, yeah. Now, can you be a chicklet and get me that corn?'

CHAPTER SEVEN

RANTING AND RAVEN

The unmistakable sound of a car getting intimately acquainted with a hedge had woken Maximilian Joseph Mallory (or MJ as he insisted his rare visitors call him) from his sleep. Tonight, as was true of every night, he had drifted off in front of his favourite programme while nursing a cup of peppermint tea.

It was less of a jolt into consciousness and more of an emersion from treacle. The living room was just as he'd left it - desperately clinging to the Seventies by the skin of its faux velvet drapes. There is no Death for interior design, but if there were, they had long been and gone.

Imitation ceiling beams drew MJ's gaze to the window in front of him. He scratched his moustache, stood up and peered past his own reflection, spying a plume of smoke rising into the inky night from the bushes at the end of his garden.

'Gosh, looks a nasty one,' he muttered with an unmistakeable Scottish twang, shoving his hand inside his dressing gown pocket for his phone. But, before he had chance to notice it was missing, his eyes refocused and his reflection gathered itself in front of him – or rather reflections.

One had its nose practically pressed against his double-glazing. The other was still sat in his armchair behind him.

'Get tae!' he shouted as he wheeled around with a sickening feeling in what used to be his stomach. He took in the full view of himself, body half-slumped in the chair. He looked like he was dreaming the most sublime dream, all lines of worry smoothed from his face, but his chest was still and his skin was ashen.

MJ wanted to believe this was all a dream, but some primal part within him knew he would never wake up. He sighed the sigh of a man who had folded at the poker table of life.

A brief moment of solemnity descended on the house and then...

'Was my nose always that hairy?' he asked his own corpse.

The sudden sound of crunching gravel outside made him jump. He hid behind the living room curtain, realising too late that his body was still sat in the armchair in full view.

'Hello?' a woman shouted from outside the front door.

For a brief moment, MJ thought his late wife Amelia had come to join him. The elation turned to fear as he realised the woman he could hear was a stranger.

'Look, I'm really sorry, I know it's late, but could you help me? I think you saw me crash my car? I just need a phone.'

'Sorry lassie,' MJ said under his breath. 'There's no one home.'

He heard her crunch-crunch round to the living room and stop. He held his breath and pulled the curtains tighter around him.

'There's no waking me up,' he smiled to himself before the sweeping beam of two headlights tracked across the room. The woman's footsteps retreated. A few minutes later, he could have sworn he heard her scream - or perhaps it was a fox in the fields. Yes, it was probably a fox.

He went back to inspecting his own dead body's nasal hair, MJ had whiled away the hours walking through his own walls.

The next morning, the sense of loss gave way to a dull acceptance that this must be his life now. He had spent the night walking back and forth through the walls I his house so decided to put his new state of being to good use. His first thought had been to take a close look at the plumbing, installed twenty years ago by his late wife's cousin Julius.

In his living years, he had been plagued by a mysterious dripping noise that seemed to come from everywhere and nowhere. He was convinced Julius had done a botched job.

So he was waist-deep in his own toilet yelling in hollow victory when he heard a knock at the door.

'Mr Mallory?'

It was the postman, Bert. They had known each other for years but he still insisted on calling MJ Mr Mallory.

MJ rushed to the door but remembered himself just in time.

'Bert?' he shouted from the hallway. 'Can you hear me?'

'Mr Mallory? I've got a parcel for you.'

Shocked to have made contact from the great beyond, MJ wasn't sure what to do next. He heard Bert's feet shuffling on the gravel as he made his way to the living room window.

'Oh no,' MJ sighed.

'Mr...Mr Mallory, are you okay?' Bert had his nose pressed against the glass, his breath fogging up the pane, as he stared at the body in the armchair.

'Uh, yes. I mean no,' MJ said, thinking on his feet as he hovered out of sight. 'I am feeling a bit ill actually, fella. Could you call an ambulance?'

'Are you sure, Mr Mallory? Only they do say to only call in an emergency and... How are you talking without moving your lips? That's amazing!'

'I really do think I'd rather get some form of emergency service in here, Bert.'

'Honestly, you should go on telly with that talent!'

'Bert!'

'No need to panic, Mr Mallory. I'll just fetch the Doc and he can come and see you, alright? Oh, and I do need a signature for this parcel if you can make it to the door.'

'No, Bert,' MJ silently cursed the vintage Atari he'd impulse-bought online, now wrapped under Bert's arm. 'Listen, I don't want to be a bother and I don't want anyone but a trained paramedic touching the body... I mean, *my body*. Do you understand? Not you, not the village GP. I don't want to frighten you.'

'Oh Mr Mallory that is sweet,' Bert stepped back from the window and walked back to the door. 'I've seen it all, you know, though,' he shouted through the letterbox. 'One time I was delivering a letter to Mrs Allcott and she answered the door covered, and I mean covered, in peanut butter.'

Bert hesitated for a moment, adjusting the parcel under his arm: 'Actually, forget I told you that Mr Mallory. She'd be mortified. She had no idea about my allergy.'

MJ rolled his eyes: 'Bert, you don't understand. I'm very cold and stiff and I think there's a good chance I've had a little accident.'

Bert chuckled: 'It's nothing to be ashamed of, Mr Mallory! I did that once – had a bit too much of the old sauce, you know. Terrible mess.'

'Bert!'

'Okay, righto! I'll fetch the doc. Sit tight, Mr Mallory.'

By the time Doris fluttered down onto the gravel drive that afternoon, a gaggle of villagers were milling around MJ's house like wasps on jam.

'Flippin' Nora,' the bird muttered as she scooted out of the way of two paramedics carrying a body bag out of the front door.

She made it through the hallway, beady eyes searching for signs of the paranormal, but there was only an excess of the living. A vicar and a locksmith were talking in the hallway.

'Do you think poor Bert's been working too hard?' the reverend asked.

'I don't understand how he had a full conversation with a man who's been dead for at least a day,' the locksmith replied, scratching his ear with a set of skeleton keys.

A woman clutching a silver pitcher scurried from the living room, so Doris quickly pretended to be an unwanted piece of taxidermy.

'What on earth is going on?' the bird whispered.

Eventually, she made it to the master bedroom. Her little talons catching on the carpet as she hopped to the bed and stopped.

There was a moment of silence and then the pink divan rippled as a hand pushed the material up to reveal a slightly translucent face that stared indignantly at the bird.

'Och, that is the last straw,' MJ said. 'Half the village is bad enough. I'm not having the local wildlife in here to boot. Shoo! Shoo!'

He crawled out from under the bed and kicked at Doris, nervously checking the doorway for signs of approaching people.

'Here, here. Get off!' Doris shrieked, flapping up to a bookshelf.

It is quite a tricky feat to master a silent scream, but MJ managed it with aplomb. He jammed both hands between his knees, as if he was bracing for a crash in an aircraft, and squeaked. Then, he hopped on one leg and pointed at Doris with his mouth open as he tried to take on board yet another bewildering sight.

'I take it you are Max Mallory?' Doris said, talons tapping on the wood. This snapped MJ to attention.

'You know my name?'

'Unfortunately, yes, it appears I do.'

She ran her beak through her glossy black feathers.

'Well,' said MJ, standing on tiptoes for a closer look at the bird. 'If you were looking to be a portent of doom, you're rather late.'

'I think you'll find you're the late one,' the raven replied as she fluttered down to MJ's shoulder. He was looking less translucent by the minute. 'This is all highly irregular but I assure you that if you bear with us things will be back on schedule shortly.'

'Talking,' spluttered MJ. 'Talking bird.'

'Yes, talking bird, sir.'

'Highly irregular.'

'Yes, sir.'

'So, this isn't normal?'

'Uh no, sir. With respect, we wouldn't usually leave a soul to cower under his bed for hours unaccompanied. It's unseemly, isn't it? Looks like we nearly lost you for a moment there, but you're looking much brighter now.'

'Well now that you mention it, this was beginning to feel like something had gone rather wrong.'

'You're jolly lucky to still be here, actually.'

'Yes, I do feel so very, very... lucky.'

There was a stomping of feet coming up the stairs and MJ darted behind the bedroom door just in time as the reverend trotted past and disappeared into the bathroom.

'Perhaps we should start with who all these people are,' continued Doris. 'Your whole house is like a joke waiting for the punch line.'

MJ sighed and rubbed his eyes in exhaustion. 'The postman brought a doctor. She could nae get in the house so she fetched a locksmith. The smith found my body and called the ambulance and then he decided to call the vicar. The vicar called my mother. My mother brought her three sisters and they brought their kids.'

'Why didn't you just pop your head out and say "Boo!"?' Doris said, spitting feathers.

'I barely spoke to half these people in life. What makes you imagine I'm suddenly going to get all talky-talky now I'm dead?'

The vicar exited the bathroom, wiped his hands on his trousers and thumped back down the stairs.

MJ's voice turned to a whisper: 'Besides, I would nae be caught dead doing anything as clichéd as saying, 'Boo!'

'Okay then,' Doris said, geeing herself up. 'Wait here, please. If there's one thing I know it's how to clear a room.'

CHAPTER EIGHT

THE AFTERWARD

For thousands of years many scholars, theologians, and professors have philosophised on the nature of life after death. Only one person in the entirety of human history has actually got it right.

Brenda Mobusi had been dusting her living room lampshade when a clear vision of The Afterward came to her and, with it, a true understanding of the meaning of life itself - or lack thereof.

No one believed her, of course.

When she died, some thirty years later, an unfortunately misspelt plaque was placed on a park bench. It read:

BRENDA'S FAVOURITE SPOT IN ALL THE
WORLD. FLY HIGH WITH THE ANGLES.

What it should have said was:

BRENDA, POSSIBLY THE MOST
SPIRITUALLY ENLIGHTENED BEING IN
THE GALAXY, ONCE ATE A SANDWICH
HERE AND MENTIONED IT, IN PASSING,
TO HER SISTER.

The Afterward had remained largely unchanged since Brenda's vision.

Towering skyscrapers threatened to pierce the clouds. They looked like pillars of pure light in the sun - sparkling with an iridescence so intense it threw fractured rainbows across the rooftops.

Max looked with wonder at a vast city in front of her, stretching off into the horizon. By some miracle she had made it to The Afterward while still clinging desperately to the last vestiges of life within her.

It almost hurt Max's eyes to look at the metropolis in front of her. It was so beautiful, but it felt dangerous as well – like staring at the sun too long. She knew in that moment she had peered behind the curtain of life and seen things she wasn't supposed to see. It made the animal part of her brain feel trapped and panicky.

'Woah,' she said.

'Quite big, isn't it?' Graham nodded.

'I mean I half expected some dystopian dump, alive with the sound of gunshots. This is stunning!'

'Blimey, has the journey thus far really shattered your illusions that much? I almost feel proud.'

'Whoever architected this place, I want to hire them to do my house,' Max said, feeling the faintness coming again.

They were stood on one of The Afterward ferry port's many viewing platforms. The streets below were thronged with people, and in every building, there was movement and life. Billboards advertised new flavours of soda, taxi horns blared and the smell of hotdogs wafted from a street vendor far below.

However, from their vantage point, everything seemed calm and muted.

'So, The Afterward is a *city*?' Max said.

'Well, this bit certainly is. I guess this is some people's idea of paradise.'

'Not yours?'

'No, give me a log cabin in the forest any day over this. You?'

'Hmm, a cottage in a village. Wildflowers in the garden, wood pigeons cooing in the trees, a view over the rolling hi...'

Once again, Max was overcome with light-headedness and she grasped the silver handrail of the balcony to steady herself. She was beginning to look pale and see-through. Instinctively, she fought the feeling knowing if she gave in to it she may never leave The Afterward.

'We need to get you out of here,' said Graham, concern carved into his stony face. 'If you're as alive as you think you are, you can't stay long or you'll go from a near-death experience to a totally dead experience. On the bright side, if the worst does happen, I can probably pull a few strings and get you that cottage.'

'Oh thanks,' Max said. 'I feel much better now.'

The pair stumbled down to the street level and through the station doors where the city suddenly felt very different. Here was the hubbub of thousands of souls marching along the pavement: - talking, singing, some even screaming at each other.

Max out into the warm air and immediately feeling her shoe squish into fresh, sticky chewing gum lying on the cut crystal pavement.

'Oh,' she said weakly, wobbling slightly. 'There's the humanity I know and tolerate!'

'I'm surprised you're surprised!' Graham said as he put his head under her arm and began supporting her down the street. 'People are people, Max – dead or alive.'

'But we were just saying how beautiful it all is.'

'They don't need any of this. The advertising, the food, the gum. It's there because it's familiar and comforting. We give you what you know and what you know is litter louts and capitalism.'

'There's no revelation then? No salvation?'

'Doesn't look like it, does it?'

'That's depressing.'

Several people in the throng of passers-by had begun to notice Graham. They pointed and whispered to each other.

'Mr Reaper, it is such a pleasure,' said a woman dressed in an Edwardian velvet gown, as she approached them sheepishly.

'I'm such a fan,' a man in a trilby behind her yelled.

Some of the fans rolled up their sleeves and presented their arms to Graham to sign as he slowly turned from white, to pink, to puce.

A sombre looking man dressed like a Roman centurion gripped his hand firmly: 'I never got a chance to thank you. You were such a comfort to me.'

'Um, you're all very kind,' Graham said hurriedly as he looked to escape from the developing huddle. 'I had no idea, really. Thank you!'

He successfully freed himself and Max from the circle, but it was clear she was becoming heavier.

'You almost looked like you were enjoying yourself there,' she whispered. 'Who are you again?'

Graham looked at Max. She looked truly ghostly now. He scooped her up and began stumbling across the road with her in his arms.

'You are Max Godwin,' he told her. 'You are not dead! You're going to be alright.'

He lurched into a quiet alleyway on the other side of the street, laid Max down on the ground and began frantically searching.

'Where is it? Where is it? Aha!'

He bent down and pulled up on the edges of a manhole cover. On it were the words 'Brooklyn N. Y. C.' There was a great noise of clanking metal as he heaved the cover up and slid it sideways over the road. A plume of hot, fetid air rose up from the uncovered hole.

'Hey, keep the noise down - I'm trying to sleep,' Max slurred, curling into the foetal position.

'No time for naps. This is our way out of here, kid.'

He ran back to Max, grabbed her arms and began pulling her towards the hole.

'Hey, get off me, you creep!' she shouted.

'I'm saving your life!'

'Help! Help!'

With one last heave, Graham pushed Max into the darkness and she fell with a long shriek of terror.

It occurred to Graham, as he put his foot on a rung of the manhole ladder, that he had not heard Max hit the bottom of the drain. Odd, he thought, considering the drop was no more than a few feet. He ducked and slid the cover back over from underneath, plunging everything into darkness.

Graham dropped his foot down to the next rung on the ladder and then reached for another, but it wasn't there. It took him by surprise and, before he knew it, he had slipped into the pitch-black with a yell.

It felt as though he were falling a great distance. Long enough to run out of breath to scream. The laws of gravity seemed to cease to apply as the wet brick walls of the tunnel went rushing by his ears. Finally, he landed with a splash on something soft and squidgy.

'What was that?' he heard Max say after some moments of silence.

Graham scrabbled over to her on his hands and knees and fumbled to hold her shoulders.

'Who am I? he asked.

'What are you doing?'

'Who am I?'

'Well, you're Graham, of course!'

'Oh my,' Graham gasped and hugged her tightly. 'I thought I'd lost you!'

'What happened? What's that smell? And why do I feel so woozy?'

'I dropped you into a New York manhole.'

'Oh...thank you?'

'I wasn't counting on the drop, obviously. Just in time though. A moment more and you would've been gone forever.'

'Now I'm sorry I asked,' Max said as Graham slowly helped her stand. 'How did you know it was the right sewer?'

'I still don't think you understand how old I am, Max. I may look like a man in his thirties…'

Max sniggered, interrupting his flow.

'Forties... LATE forties! But I'm as old as human civilisation, older than Neanderthals. I helped draw up the plans for this place. We built access tunnels so we could reach each other.'

'We?' Max said, wobbling on her feet.

'The four horsemen, Max. This line connects up to Brooklyn. Just a short walk through human excrement and you'll be back in the fresh air.'

They made their way slowly through the sewer, illuminated by little clusters of glowing, green mushrooms dotting the sides of the tunnel. Echoes of dripping water followed them as they made their way slowly onward.

Despite slipping and sliding in the darkness, Max declined Graham's offer of a light. Some things were better left unknown.

'What's in New York, then?' Max asked.

'Lennie.'

'Cute name.'

'Don't be fooled, he's as slimy as they come. Lennie's short for Pestilence.'

'So this...oh steady... Lennie guy,' Max said as she skidded on slippery things on the tunnel floor. 'What does he have to do with anything?'

'He's...oh, that was close... like the king of disease.'

'One of the four riders?'

'Mm, very good. War, Pestilence, Famine and...whoa nelly... little old me. You said you swerved to avoid a rat on the road when you crashed?'

'Yes.'

'Well there isn't a rat in the world that isn't under Lennie's command.'

'What do diseases have to do with rats?'

'Everything.'

'That seems a bit... argh... unfair, Graham. Isn't that rattist?'

Max frantically scraped her shoe on the tunnel wall and retched, but with every step she felt her colour returning.

'Leptospirosis...oops...Hantavirus, salmonella. The actual... wahey... Black Death,' Graham coughed in disgust as he slipped on something both soft and sticky.

'And you think Lennie's responsible for this whole mess somehow?'

'I'm not really sure what to think. Lennie is a very self-serving being. He likes filth and rats and that's about it. It would take a lot for him to act out. Either way, he's tied up in all this and I'm going to find out how.'

CHAPTER NINE

PLAGUED WITH GUILT

Leonard Pescht sat in the cab of his ancient white truck. A cigarette perched perilously on the edge of his lip – teetering back and forth with every breath. He squinted through the flecked bug entrails on his windscreen and waited.

A leaf, gilded with fiery orange and yellow, twirled through the air and landed on the truck bonnet. It obscured the face of a cartoon rat framed by the words "Pescht Control, NYC".

'Brooklyn is beautiful in the fall,' Lennie muttered.

He arched one eyebrow as he ran a hand through his greasy black hair. He turned all his attention to the leaf. Its colours faded under his scornful gaze - brown and then black before the wind took it as a pile of dust, scattering it along the street like ashes.

A shocked screech pierced the thick soup of city noise and Lennie grinned. He opened the truck door just a crack and a large black rat jumped inside, crawled up his trousers and perched on his shoulder.

'Nice work,' Lennie said, tickling the rat behind its sticky ear. Its fur was oily in places and its pink skin was visible underneath its fluff. Lennie shifted in his seat. He had barely rolled the truck around the block for a few minutes when a man in chef's whites, sweat running down his forehead, sprinted out of a café. He was waving a tea towel to flag Lennie down.

The rat disappeared into the footwell as Lennie wound the window down and smiled. His stained teeth poked through his shrivelled lips.

'Geez, I can't believe this! I just saw you driving by. Lucky me!' the chef said, chuckling nervously. 'Please, you gotta help me, man. I got rats in the kitchen. I can't serve.'

'Well, I don't know, sir,' Lennie said, shrugging and picking at a crusted stain on his trousers. 'I'm a busy man, you know? I got this job in Queens in an hour...'

'PLEASE! I'm desperate, man. I've called every pest controller I know. None of 'em can see me for two days. I'll pay whatever.'

'Well, sir,' Lennie's smile spread like an oil spill across his stubbled face. 'Out of the goodness of my heart, I think we can come to an arrangement.'

Max felt the fluffy fibres of the dressing gown brush against her cheek as she stretched out on the king-size bed. Graham was showering in the bathroom. She could hear him humming the Danse Macabre, occasionally punctuated by an expletive as he found another smattering of something hideous in his crevices.

'I know we're in a rush,' he shouted to her, 'but I was absolutely not going to spend the rest of this journey smelling like a toilet.'

'Glad you've got your priorities straight!' said Max, rolling her eyes.

Graham shouted again: 'What? Did you say something?'

He appeared from behind the door with a towel wrapped around his head and a serene smile on his face. He was wearing an "I love N.Y." T-shirt hurriedly grabbed from a stall across the street. His beloved sweater was now lying at the bottom of a bin. He had rested it there gently and placed an affectionate hand upon it in thanks for its service. He had only bought it a century ago.

'Better?' Max asked.

'Better,' he said, unplugging his phone from a charger on the nightstand. 'How about you? Feeling a bit less dead?'

Max nodded.

Graham sat on the bed: 'The evidence is irrefutable, isn't it? I'm sorry, Max.'

'Graham Reaper, was that you apologising?'

'I mean it, Max. Complacency got the better of me. I didn't take you seriously. There's a warm body waiting out there for you.'

'Thank you? And gross,' Max said.

'So, are you wearing it?'

Max parted her dressing gown to reveal that she had a matching T-shirt on and Graham gave her an excited thumbs-up of approval.

They made their way out of the hotel via the service elevator. It took them down into the hubbub of the clattering kitchen. No one batted an eye as they pushed through a squeaky fire door and found themselves in a small alley littered with industrial-sized bins. Steam curled in plumes out of giant vents and tangled around fire escapes stretching up to the roof line. There were a million smells all blended together, including hotdogs, laundry, rotting vegetables and rainwater.

'Right then,' Graham said, readying himself.

He crept up to an enormous bin and shoved his hand inside without hesitation.

'Eurrrrggh! You literally just had a shower!' Max winced.

Slowly Graham withdrew his clenched fist. He was holding a rat as large as a small terrier – greasy, brown and angry.

He grinned and waved it at Max.

'Nope. Nope. No thank you,' she said, stepping backwards until she was up against a brick wall.

'Hey! Hey!' the rat said. 'Watch the fur! Watch the fur!'

Max retched: 'And it talks. Marvellous.'

'Where is Lennie?' Graham asked the rat, his eyes narrowing.

'How should I know?' the rat shrugged, raising its paws in mock ignorance. 'The boss goes where he pleases!'

'Wrong answer. Perhaps you'd like me to introduce you to a nearby cat?'

'Please, no. I don't take too well to felines,' the rat said as it squirmed in Graham's hand.

'Here kitty, kitty, kitty,' Graham said softly.

there was a rustle of cardboard and a tomcat appeared from behind a bin further along the alley.

Graham smiled as the cat approached: 'You're never far away from a hungry moggy in New York City. Oh, this one looks starving…'

The rat shrieked.

'Uh, listen,' it giggled nervously. 'Maybe I misspoke there?'

'Maybe you did.'

'Maybe a buddy said he'd be in the Bronx today.'

'If I find out you lied to me I'll serve you up to this kitty in a hot dog bun. Understand?'

The rat nodded frantically as Graham bent down to release it. No sooner had it felt Graham's grip loosen, it scampered away and into a drain without looking back. The cat looked terribly disappointed.

'Tell him Graham's coming for a quiet word,' Graham shouted after the rodent, his voice echoing back at him from the darkness.

They walked out of the alley and the cat followed.

'Don't wipe your bin juice hands on your lovely new T-shirt, Graham,' Max despaired.

'Where am I supposed to wipe them then?!' he protested.

'Hey, your pocket's ringing,' Max said, shivers still running up and down her body.

He picked it up.

'Graham?' Azrael squealed in a whisper. 'I'm hiding in the office stationery cupboard.'

A pack of highlighters fell roughly on her head. 'Graham. Oh…Graham. WHERE HAVE YOU BEEN?'

'I'm sorry. Listen, Azrael,' Graham took a deep breath. 'I messed up a few days ago in Chudleigh. I thought I'd picked up Max Mallory, but I've actually got someone called Max Godwin. I'm an idiot.'

'Yes, I know, Graham. Not that you're an idiot – although, of course, you are. I know about Max.'

'You know?'

'Yes, I sent Doris to Chudleigh and she found the other Max cowering under a divan in a house so full of characters it looked like a game of Cluedo. She's been watching him since yesterday. We're jolly lucky we got to him in time. The system thinks you've already picked him up so no-one knows he's missing.'

'Have you told anyone?'

'Not yet, no. I've been trying to talk to you first.'

'That's not all of it though. I think Max G is definitely not dead.'

'That's what Doris said too. I don't have a Max Godwin on my list, Graham.'

'Neither do I,' he admitted, glancing across at Max who was busy searching for a scrap of food to feed the cat. 'I think I've been set-up.'

'By whom?'

'I'm not sure, but I think Lennie's involved.'

'There was me thinking you'd had some kind of revelation,' Azrael said. 'You just messed up, Graham, and that's okay! There's no conspiracy.'

'Max's car crash happened because of a rat.'

'Oh. Well... that is suspicious.'

'I know I need to get back to the job, but I need to fix this first. How many are waiting?'

'About 40,000.'

'Is that all? Blimey, that's better than I thought.'

'No Graham, you don't understand – they've replaced you... Graham?'

Graham zoned out for a moment in shock. He would never have believed it possible they could actually replace him.

'It gets worse,' Azrael grimaced.

'Worse?'

'Your replacement is a... chicken man... or a man chicken. I'm not sure which. Either way, he's a supreme corporate pillock and the board absolutely loves him.'

'A chicken man?'

'Yes. A chicken transformed into a human. It wears a suit. It's called Simon.'

Max and Graham had gone a considerable distance along the Grand Concourse before he managed to regulate his breathing. In the meantime, a collection of cockroaches had developed a head cold and an alligator living in the sewer below (flushed down a toilet some ten years previously) got a hangnail.

'A chicken, Max! A chicken!'

Max patted Graham on the shoulder: 'Perhaps he's just better at keeping abreast of the job?'

'Alright, laugh it up. Get it all out of your system.'

'I'm sure it's running like cluckwork over there.'

'You can cluck off, how's about that?'

Graham marched ahead, half-smiling in spite of himself. He cocked his ear to a nearby storm drain and listened for the sound of tiny rodent feet.

Max was watching him with great curiosity when an old woman with permed, candy-pink hair came tottering up to her. She grabbed Max by the arms.

'Oh my stars!' she said in a thick New York accent as a string of pearls jittered around her neck. 'Did you see the size of that rat just now? Thank heavens for that pest controller. I'm getting out of here.'

'Wait, where?' Max shouted as the old lady power-walked up the street and pointed down an alley without looking.

Max looked where the woman had gestured.

'Hey, don't I....' she turned back, but the woman was gone. '...know you?'

She yelled for Graham instead, his head now fully inside the drain. 'I think I know the way.'

They came across Lennie's white van all too quickly – but Lennie himself was nowhere to be seen. Max peered into the window and made direct eye contact with a rat in the passenger seat.

'Take a picture, it'll last longer,' it squeaked.

'Charming,' sniffed Max.

The mud-caked truck was parked outside a derelict café. Two smashed windows flanked the doorway. Graham and Max took a breath, pushed the doors open and stepped into the gloom within. As their eyes adjusted, the scene developed in front of them like a Polaroid. There were around twenty tables and every one of them was weighed down with dozens of rats. In fact, there were rats everywhere – on the chairs, scuttling across the floor, on the dusty lampshades, and hanging off the frames of faded photos nailed to the wood-panelled walls.

At the very back of the room was an old glass counter - presumably for displaying cakes and pastries, but now stuffed with rodents.

On top of it, sat cross-legged, was Lennie. He jumped off the counter with a thud.

'Look, my friends,' he sneered. 'We have guests!'

He spat on the floor at the sight of Graham and Max.

'Nice,' Max muttered.

'That is the very least of it,' Graham said under his breath. He moved forwards and produced a smile entirely too big for his face. 'Lennie, it's been too long.'

He extended a hand for Lennie but changed his mind and retracted it almost immediately.

'Well, well, well,' Lennie sniffed, wiping his nose on his crusted sleeve. 'If it isn't my buddy, Mr Reaper. To what do I owe the pleasure? Word is you've had a rough couple of days.'

He grinned, lips pulling back to reveal his stained teeth.

'It has been...unusual,' Graham nodded.

'I had a bet going with my friends here to see how long it would take you to mess up,' Lennie said with a laugh like a clogged drain.

The assembled rats squeaked and squealed loudly in acknowledgment.

'I wonder if they'd be interested to know the odds were in your favour, Len?' said Graham, slowly making his way to the counter.

Lennie picked up a banana and peeled it. With every bite he took, the fruit grew more and more brown until it was a rotten sludge dripping from his mouth.

'I don't know what you mean,' he slobbered. 'Imagine,' he turned to Max. 'The great Pale Rider taken down a peg or two. I've been waiting for this day. Come here looking for help, did you? Hoping kind old Lennie will bail you out and reap some souls?'

'Was that your plan?' Graham said. 'Throw everything off the rails and step into my shoes? It would be a real shame, Lennie, because the stench of disease suits you so well.'

'He's so mean, ain't he?' Lennie said to Max. He turned his attention back to Graham: 'I don't know if you've heard, but the last few years have been particularly bumper ones for me and my crew here! I haven't had this much fun since the Spanish Flu. So why would I want your stinking job?'

Max stared into Lennie's bloodshot eyes: 'I hope it was you,' she said, gesturing to Graham who looked confused.

Max continued: 'I mean talk about too big for your boots! High and mighty Death – didn't take much to trip him up!'

Lennie snorted: 'Hey, where did ya find this dame, Graham? I like her!'

Max moved past Graham and winked at him as she spoke to Lennie: 'I think he deserved to be humbled, don't you? He has the audacity to start slacking on the job. He got lazy, he got arrogant, looked down on you.'

'You know it was easy,' Lennie laughed. 'Just a little nudge from one of my friends here and his world came apart. And the best part is everyone blames him!'

Max laughed back with a slightly crazed look in her eyes: 'What kind of a nudge, Lennie?'

'Oh, this is the beautiful part! I sent one of my English compatriots to crash this dumb mortal nobody's car. Apparently, the look on her face was quite the picture.'

'You know what, Lennie?' Max said, moving as close to him as her nose could stand: 'I haven't introduced myself yet, have I? How rude. I'm dumb, mortal nobody.'

She lunged at Lennie without warning as his eyes widened in realisation. Before he could run she had punched him in the eye.

'Get her off me!' he yelled at Graham.

'What's that?' he said. 'The White Rider wants a helping hand from Death?'

Max yelled, landing another punch, this time on Lennie's nose.

'Yes, yes! Get her off!' Lennie screamed.

Max ceased flailing her fists and stood back, tears streaming down her face as her pent up bewilderment and rage hung heavy in the air.

'Tell us everything,' Graham said. 'You didn't just knock Max off the road for no reason, did you? How did you know two people called Max would be in the same place. How did you know I would reach her first? How did you know the crash would be enough to, what, put Max in a coma? Is that what's happened?'

'It wasn't me!' Lennie said.

'LENNIE?'

'I SWEAR! I got a call, okay?'

'FROM WHO?'

'Sybil!'

'Sybil?!'

'Yes, yes! She asked me a favour – you don't decline a favour from Sybil. She told me what do, where and when – I wrote it down, so's I wouldn't forget.'

'What are you talking about?' Max said. 'She told you what to do and you did it, why would you need a memo?'

'Oh, this is so much worse than you know.'

'Explain,' Graham said.

'She called me about seventy years ago.'

Max took a step backwards. 'But that was before I was born. Way before.'

'Before Max Mallory was born too.'

'I...' Max covered her head with her hands and crouched down for a second. 'This was my destiny before I was even born. Before my mum was born?!'

Shaking with anger, Max turned on her heel and ran out of the café.

'Ooops,' Lennie sniggered.

'I'd watch it,' Graham said. 'Or she'll come back in here and give you another black eye.'

He marched swiftly outside and began walking after Max, closely followed by Lennie.

'Max, stop – we can't be separated, remember? Doris isn't here to keep you safe anymore.'

'Why does it matter?' Max said, whirling around. 'My purpose has been fulfilled, right? So just leave me here to drift away.'

'I'm not going to do that, Max.'

'Why?'

'Because I care about you, kid,' Graham blurted, surprising even himself. 'I don't know what it was exactly that sealed all our fates. We'll never know. But I'm certain you're still alive. Everyone knows how their life started, Max, but this isn't how it ends.'

'But you don't understand, Graham. Mum told me she didn't mean to get pregnant. I was loved sure, but she was young. She met this guy in a bar and boom! There I was. Said she couldn't bring herself to do the unthinkable. But she was always going to have me, right? It was predestined.'

Graham looked back at her in stunned silence. For once lost for words.

'Because her little girl was going to crash her car on a Tuesday evening in Chudleigh thirty years later,' Max said, big, wet tears running down her cheeks.

Graham reached out to comfort her, but Max swatted him away.

'You know, Mum always told me she named me after her grandad. She loved him so much. But I guess she was wrong. She named me Max so I could get mixed up with some random guy who died in his stupid cottage in the same stupid village.'

'That's not true, Max!'

'Sounds pretty spot on to me,' Lennie beamed.

'Nobody asked you,' Graham replied.

Max looked at the two of them: 'You're as bad as each other.'

With that, she turned around and stormed up the street.

'Wait, Max!' Graham ran after her.

Lennie laughed, a dry rasping chuckle as if his lungs were made of paper. 'See you around, big brother!'

CHAPTER TEN

DEATH ON SWIFT WINGS

The sun was beginning to cool as Max and Graham hunkered down behind a stack of pallets outside the perimeter fence at LaGuardia airport as.

'Can we not just zip off to Florida in your magic van?' Max huffed. The long walk, which she had spent several paces ahead of Graham, had taken the sting out of her, but she was still filled with anger.

'Again, it's not 'magic;,' Graham said wearily. 'It's a manipulation of time and space, as per my divine right as the manifestation of death. And no, we can't just zip anywhere, because I left my magic... I left my van on the ferry, remember? I miss my van.'

Up ahead was a chain-link fence and beyond it, all manner of vehicles and people pottered back and forth like bees in a hive. In this case, many of the bees appeared to be armed.

'So we catch the next 747 out of here, then?' said Max, eying up a row of dazzling white planes in the distance.

'Oh, sure. Why don't we pop into duty free while we're waiting? Pick up a crossword, a funny neck pillow, and bottle of discount perfume. You know a flight to Florida takes about three hours, don't you? We don't have that kind of time. I need to start putting everything back the way it was pronto before chicken boy gets any big ideas.'

'Why Florida?' Max said.

'That's where Sybil lives.'

'And she chooses to live there because?'

'She really loves alligators. Why does any old person move to Florida? It's warm and it's cheap.'

'So, if we're not flying, why did you bring me to an airport?'

'Ah,' Graham smiled. 'I didn't say we weren't flying. We're taking a roc.'

He stood up and started marching away alongside the fence as if this needed no further explanation. Max shook her head and ran to catch up with him.

'A rock?' she asked. 'Not usually known for their aerodynamic qualities.'

'No,' Graham replied. 'A *roc*. Come on.'

'That's what I just said.'

They rounded a corner and Max spotted a gate in the distance with a little hut beside it. There was a golf buggy parked on the other side of the fence and someone was sitting in the driver's seat.

'I need a flight to Florida,' Graham said, leaning louchely on the ledge of the hut's glassless window.

'Yes, sir,' said the attendant inside, who bore a striking resemblance to a hospital porter in Swindon. 'My name's Todd by the way – thank you for asking.'

'I need a flight, not a helping of sass, Todd.'

'A bit of politeness goes a long way, sir.'

'I need a flight to Florida… please,' Graham grimaced.

'There now, was that so hard? There's a carrier available to go in about five hours.'

'No, I need to go right now,' Graham said, leaning in and craning his neck as he tried to see the screen. Max slowly took several steps backwards and scanned the fence on both sides for a way in.

'No can do, I'm afraid,' Todd said, turning the screen away from Graham's gaze. 'There's a flight departing in five hours, as I said, sir. Or there's another one tomorrow morning. Take your pick.'

'Look,' Graham said with a smile that could freeze forest fires. 'I hate to play this card, but you do know who I am, right?'

'Yes, I do, sir,' Todd replied, pushing up his glasses.

'Okay, so when is the next flight?'

'In five hours, sir.'

'LOOK –'

Graham was interrupted by something on the other side of the fence catching his eye. It was Max, frantically directing him to a hole in the chain-link, to the far left of the hut.

Graham coughed: 'Look, you're doing a great job. I was out of line there. Keep it up.'

Todd blinked in confusion, yet the warm fuzzy feeling in his stomach suggested he had done the right thing. He resumed clacking jovially on his keyboard.

'Good day, sir,' he said without looking up.

Graham squirmed through the hole in the fence and raced to find Max who was now sat in the back of the golf cart.

'Ah hello, inspector,' she said, as Graham shot her a puzzled expression.

'I was just explaining to the driver here,' she continued, 'that you're completing an unscheduled appraisal of the airfield today.'

'Uh, yes,' Graham said, cottoning on. 'I need to see the roc hangar immediately.'

'Of course, of course,' Max said flamboyantly. She jerked her head in the direction of the back seat. 'Well, what are you waiting for? Get in then.'

Graham climbed in behind Max, squeezing his long legs behind her seat. The buggy driver turned to meet Graham's eye.

'Hello there!' he beamed. He looked almost identical to the Todd in the ticket booth except for a pair of thick-rimmed glasses.

'Woah,' Graham said as he stared back at the booth in confusion. 'How did you...?'

'My colleague and I are minions of Apoco, sir,' the driver explained. 'I hope we haven't unsettled you with our appearance. We are very similar.'

'Hello?' Max barked. 'Time is money. To the hangar, please!'

The buggy lurched forward as Todd number three put his foot down on the accelerator.

Graham leaned forward and whispered in Max's ear: 'Do you have the slightest clue what you're doing?'

'No. Do you, Mr "Don't You Know Who I Am"?'

'Point made,' Graham said, and leaned back in his seat.

The little cart sped across the runway - its wheels throwing up dust as it hummed over the concrete. Growing ever closer was a gigantic aircraft hangar with equally huge, double doors closed shut against a gentle breeze.

The buggy came to a halt outside and Graham and Max climbed out.

'Thank you very much,' Max said to the driver. 'Todd, right?'

Todd looked visibly shocked: 'No way, how did you guess?'

'Just a hunch,' she smiled. 'I'll be sure to mention your good work to the management.'

'Wow, thank you, miss,' he said. He tipped his cap, pressed his foot to the pedal, and and zipped off back to the entrance.

The hangar doors looked even more imposing up close. The hinges alone were the size of double-decker buses.

The first hint of a rain shower fell on Max's face as she stared up in awe: 'How are we ever going to get in?'

'Now, that I do know,' Graham replied with confidence. He walked a few short steps past Max and pushed on the towering door. To her surprise, he disappeared inside. Then she noticed that there was, in fact, a much smaller, person-sized door cut into the larger one.

She lifted a foot to step in but, before she could cross the threshold, Graham popped his head back out of the shadowy interior.

'Just to say, don't scream,' he said.

'Eh?' Max said, foot hovering mid-step.

'It's just she's quite big and she tends to have that effect on people.'

'Who does?'

'The roc.'

'Yes, you keep saying that as if I'm supposed to know what it is!'

Graham gently directed Max inside the hangar, his hand poised aloft to muffle her screams if necessary. Nothing could have prepared her for the sight that met her eyes.

Stood in the middle of the hangar was an eagle of monstrous proportions. Her head was easily the size of an average two-bed terraced house. Her talons would have no trouble grasping an elephant. Her gleaming brown feathers were as big as palm fronds.

The roc's head bent slightly as she preened herself, her sharp beak clicking like a round of applause as it slid down each feather.

Max slowly and purposefully backed out of the door and into the now pouring rain with Graham following behind.

'Hell's teeth!' she shouted as Graham frantically shushed her. 'That's not 'quite big'! It's planetary!'

'SHE,' Graham said, 'is an old friend. One of the last great titans of ancient history. She's in The Arabian Nights! A genuine legend.'

'Oh good. I'll remember to ask for her autograph.'

'She's our only ticket out of here in time, Max.'

'That's because her wings stretch from here to Orlando. I've only even been on an aeroplane once!'

'Well, if you can do economy class on a jumbo jet this should be a piece of cake.'

The roc was already watching them intently when they re-entered the hangar. Graham wedged the door shut behind them with a scaffolding pole through the crash bar.

'A genuine legend?' the bird boomed with a voice like velvet. 'Graham, I'm touched.'

'Forgot about your super hearing, Guthrie,' Graham blushed as he linked arms with Max and forced her closer.

'Guthrie?' Max said through her teeth.

The bird laughed and bent her head down until it rested with a floor-shaking thud on the ground. 'I chose it myself, little spirit. It means windy place. Funny, no?'

Max stared at Guthrie's eye, a swimming pool of liquid gold suspended in crystal with a fathomless black centre.

'Gosh, you're beautiful,' she said, her fear giving way to admiration.

'As are you, Max. For a human, of course.'

'Guthrie, I need a favour,' Graham said as he grabbed a couple of thick aviator jackets from a peg on the wall nearby.

'I know, I heard that too. Need a word with Sybil, do you? In my experience she usually comes to you.'

Max gulped: 'Can we not just have a web chat with this Sybil lady?'

'Come on,' Graham scoffed. 'One doesn't Zoom call the decider of human destiny.'

'Why not?'

'She doesn't know how to work a mobile phone.'

'You know I could get in a lot of trouble for this, Graham,' Guthrie said. 'I'm due to fly out on a job in five hours.'

'It's literally a matter of life or death.'

'Well, in that case, you'd best grab that ladder and hop aboard Roc Airlines.'

Graham turned around and spotted a warehouse ladder. He wheeled it slowly over to Guthrie's head and held out a hand for Max.

'May I?' he said.

From outside the hangar there was a sound of skidding golf cart wheels.

'This feels like a bad idea,' Max said.

'Got any better ones?' Graham replied.

Guthrie blinked: 'Time is a factor.'

Someone was now attempting to ram the hangar door open. With a start, Max grabbed Graham's hand and began running up the ladder. When she reached the top she leapt off the platform and onto Guthrie's silken neck feathers. Graham was right behind her. Slowly they pulled themselves up behind Guthrie's head.

The great bird stood up suddenly and Max felt her stomach drop as they rose up through the air. She and Graham screeched in fear.

'Sorry!' Guthrie gasped. 'Should've given you a warning!'

'Not filling me with confidence,' Max said as she hurriedly pulled on her jacket on and buried her fingers in the bird's plumage.

Suddenly the hangar's little door burst open. The Todds ran in. The look of fear on their faces suggested they had thought no further than entering the hangar.

'Alright, hold it there,' one of them squeaked ineffectually as the other one sporting suspiciously wet trousers ran and hid

Guthrie hooked her beak around the edge of one of the huge hangar doors and peeled it back like a giant tin of tuna. The other door followed with little resistance.

'Did I mention I've only flown once before?' Max shouted as the Roc broke into a run. She flapped her titanic wings, buffeting Max and Graham with great gusts of wet, cold air. Max felt Guthrie's warmth under her hands and pressed her cheek to the heat. Beneath her, she could hear the bird's feet pounding as they picked up speed. The wind and thundering pace combined were almost deafening. Then, suddenly, there was silence. Max could hear the wind rushing over their heads. She looked sideways and saw one of Guthrie's wings stretching out in front of her. The clouds rolled over it like candy floss. Then the wet spray of mist gave way to hot sun as they broke through the rain and into a different world.

The bird was soon gliding over North Carolina, head pointing like an arrow into the wind as she sliced through the sky.

'I could get used to this,' Max grinned, clinging to Guthrie's quills with white knuckles.

CHAPTER ELEVEN

A FATE WORSE THAN DEATH

On a quiet, tree-lined avenue in Florida, Canities Retirement Home squatted like an ungainly dog caught short in the woods.

The bright white walls of the three-storey house were blinding in the mid-morning sun. Two bay windows, dressed in net curtains, teased a glimpse into the life beyond. Little lizards flecked the borders of the front path. It was the last place you would expect to find any supernatural goings-on and that was sort of the point.

Max was sat in the living room, her hair still windswept and jagged from the flight. She could hear jazz music wafting from one of the many rooms. There was also the sound of a busy kitchen filled with banging pots and bubbling pans competing with the music and sometimes, strangely, complementing it. The smell of overcooked soup, talcum powder, and old books was seeping out of the walls.

An elderly lady shuffled in. She was wearing very stylish high-waisted trousers and a bright, stripy jumper. Her silver hair was pinned up in curls. She perched on a giant floral armchair as if she feared it might explode if she made any sudden moves. A male carer in a nurse's uniform followed close behind and knelt beside her.

'Hello dear,' the old woman said with a strong Southern twang. She was looking straight at Max and nodding. Max's eyes widened and she opened her mouth to speak.

'Hello Phyllis,' the carer replied and Max relaxed.

'Are you visiting someone?' Phyllis asked.

'No,' the carer replied. 'I work here, hun, remember?'

Max, feeling like an intruder, turned away and looked at the fireplace,. There were birthday cards on the mantle and she squinted to see the age. Graham was taking longer to check on Sybil's whereabouts than he had thought.

'I said are you visiting someone?' Phyllis said again, but louder.

The carer raised his voice too: 'Yes, and I said…'

'No, not you, dear,' Phyllis interrupted soothingly. 'The pretty, young lady over there.'

Max turned back and their eyes met. The old woman raised a finger and pointed directly at her.

'Oh Phyllis,' said the carer. 'There's no one there.'

For just a few seconds all sound in the room melted into nothing as Max realised she was being looked at by live, human eyes for the first time in three days.

She waved: 'You can see me?'

'I've always had the sight, child. Since I was a little girl. Some can see and some can't.'

Phyllis smiled. Her powdered face crinkled softly like floured pizza dough.

The carer patted her on the arm with a concerned look on his face: 'I'll get you an iced tea and your meds.'

He left the room hurriedly, muttering under his breath.

Phyllis watched him leave and checked he had turned the corner of the corridor.

'They already think I'm losing my mind,' she chuckled, stroking the string of pearls around her neck. 'One more "episode" won't hurt me.'

'Oh, sorry,' Max said. 'Should I have said something sooner? I just assumed…'

'No, don't be silly,' Phyllis said, waving her hand. 'If I forgot one of their names or tripped on the carpet, they'd still say I'm losing my marbles. People have been thinking I'm crazy since I was thirteen years old!'

'I..'

'That's when I saw my first spirit. A man stopped outside our yard and asked for directions. Then your friend Graham appeared on a pale green horse. I'd never seen anything like it.'

Graham came barrelling into the room and realised he was interrupting: 'Oh hello! Making friends, are we?'

'Speak of the devil,' Phyllis said.

'You used to ride a horse?' Max asked him.

'Of course – in my younger days. Or we would've been the four designated drivers of the apocalypse, wouldn't we? It was murder on my coccyx.'

He gestured towards the door: 'Ready to go?'

Max rose to her feet: 'Goodbye, Phyllis. It was a pleasure to meet you.'

'Goodbye, dear. Keep your chin up, I'm sure everything will be okay in the end.' She turned her attention to Graham: 'Some other time, dear.'

'He smiled: 'You can count on it.'

She waved sweetly as Max and Graham left the room and walked down the corridor.

'Do you know when you'll see her again?' Max asked him.

'I'm afraid not. A person's destiny is Sybil's domain, remember? Speaking of which, she's at home, apparently. Let's go pay her a visit.'

Past the kitchen and down a slope, a set of French doors led out to a beautiful lawn. The Florida heat smacked Max in the face like a hot wall as the air conditioning kissed her goodbye.

'Why could Phyllis see you?' Max asked.

'Some people are just a bit more tuned in,' Graham nodded, beads of sweat trickling down his nose. 'Most of the time they're called crazy and locked away in dark places. It's a habit of humanity.'

They marched along the flower-bordered path.

'Sybil's in number twenty-three,' Graham said.

An army of bungalows stretched into the distance in front of them, as if poised to march into battle. Each one sported some kind of plastic accessory - a squirrel, a butterfly, a mooning gnome.

It took them some time to find the right house. The door was painted blue and it had a frosted glass window. It felt ancient and modern all at once.

'Just for the record,' Graham whispered. 'Sybil knew we would be here at this exact moment. So all of what's coming is pure theatrics. She always did love the drama.'

Right on cue, a light flicked on inside and a shape began to form behind the glass - amorphous at first, but becoming clearer and larger. Then the door burst open and an old woman with huge pink sunglasses, curly pink hair and a hint of a Greek accent exclaimed: 'You're a minute late this time! Come in, come in!'

'This time?' Max said.

'What did I just say?' Graham sighed.

'Stupid boy,' Sybil cackled. 'I say 'this time', my dear, because you've made this journey before and you'll make it again about five-thousand different ways and counting.'

Max tried hard to recall her A-Level physics.

'Alternate timelines, petal,' Sybil said. 'Don't fret it. It'll only make your nose bleed.'

Max had a sudden realisation that made her stop in her tracks. Sybil looked her dead in the eyes and elbowed Graham sharply in the ribs: 'She's going to get it quicker this time though.'

'I've already met you!' Max said. 'You were in The Bronx – you told me where to find Lennie!'

Sybil nodded: 'Actually, flower, you've seen me twice. The lady on the moped at the ferry terminal? Tally-ho?'

Graham and Max's eyes widened at the same time. Graham pinched his nose in exasperation: 'You've been prodding us along this whole time?'

'I would say gently guiding,' Sybil smiled.

Graham tutted: 'Yes, you would, wouldn't you?'

She beckoned them through a claustrophobic hall and into a yellow-walled living room. 'Sometimes Fate just has to intervene once or twice, no?'

The room was decorated like every era in history had a fight and then sat down for a rest. An Art Deco lamp was slumped beside a mid-century modern armchair, while a Renaissance mirror propped itself up beside a Roman gladiator mask.

'You'll have a seat,' Sybil said with an air of inevitability and all three plopped down on a beige Nineties sofa.

'You know why we've come,' Graham said.

'You've come,' said Sybil, crossing her legging-clad legs, 'to get me to tell you what you already know. What a foolish endeavour.'

'You wanted to teach Graham a lesson,' Max said. 'And you almost killed me to do it.'

'Well, you came quite close in The Afterward, but you're still with us,' Sybil said, leaning over and pinching Max's cheek. 'You're rather angry with me.'

Max had been squeezing the throw pillow beside her so tightly she had lost the feeling in her hand.

Sybil continued: 'Let's not pretend you haven't benefitted from this, though.'

Graham stepped in: 'I don't think that's fair! I've been dragging her around for days – I nearly finished her off for good. How is that a benefit?'

'But you didn't,' Sybil replied calmly as she turned back to Max. 'You were working a job you hated, you never spoke to anyone but your mother. You were deeply unhappy, pumpkin. This experience is a gift. You're going to appreciate life more, be bolder, be braver because of what you've gone through here.'

The journey with Graham flashed through Max's mind and she realised, with annoyance, she could'nt argue.

'You're welcome,' Sybil smiled.

'I didn...'

'Yes. You did.'

'What about him then?' Max blurted, pointing at Graham, who was staring out of the window.

He took a deep breath and scratched his head: 'Sounds a lot like me, doesn't it? I hated my job. I never spoke to anyone.'

'Death,' Sybil said to Max, 'is the axis on which the whole world turns. Without him everything turns to chaos.'

'So Fate intervened,' Max said.

Sybil grinned: No need to thank me.'

'On balance,' Graham said, 'I would have preferred a quiet word in a café instead.'

'You didn't listen,' Sybil said calmly. 'You needed to be shown. In every universe, in every scenario, every timeline, this was the only way.'

'Well congratulations, I guess?' Graham said blankly. 'I now want nothing more than to get back to doing my job.'

'Brilliant,' Sybil said, clapping her hands together as she stood up. 'Now, if you don't mind, I've got a poker game to win in the dining hall.'

'No, not brilliant,' Graham harrumphed. 'As you well know, Sybil, I've been replaced by a chicken and your meddling has convinced the board I'm not to be trusted.'

'Well, I guess that's the end of it then,' Sybil said.

'There has to be a way back in, surely?'

'Do you want a way back in?' Sybil smiled.

'You know, as Fate personified, you sure do rely on other people to do the heavy lifting,' Max said.

Sybil laughed: 'Damn straight, petal!'

CHAPTER TWELVE

ON THE SCRAPHEAP

Azrael was snoring softly at her desk. Every breath made the pages of the well-worn notebook beside her flutter back and forth. The sun was only just beginning to rise. She had fallen asleep at her desk – under the circumstances, going home had felt even more uncomfortable than seven hours in an office chair.

From the car park there suddenly came an ear-splitting scream. Azrael snapped upright, drool still clinging to the corner of her mouth.

'COCK-A-DOODLE-DOOOOOOOOO!'

She spun around in her chair and looked out through the window to see Simon jumping down from a bike rack and straightening his tie.

She checked the clock and realised with horror that it was 5am. Wheezing in disbelief, she gingerly made her way to the staff kitchen for a very big cup of coffee. By the time she returned Simon was pacing the room and repeatedly combing his hair.

'Morning, Simon.'

'Mm? Oh yes, morning! Morning, morning, morning.'

'Are you doing okay there?'

'Fine. Fine. Top stuff.'

'I think you've combed enough now, Simon.'

He stopped brushing his locks and let his hand fall. Azrael took a sip of coffee and walked around to face him.

'You know this is more of a remote working deal, don't you? You don't have to be here.'

But as she met Simon's eyes she realised he was weeping.

'What is this?' he asked miserably, gesturing weakly to his eyes.

'What? Your tears?'

'Yes! The salty water. Make it stop.'

'I can't. You're the only one who can do that.'

'Why is it happening?'

'Some people cry when they're happy…'

She looked into Simon's baleful eyes. 'But I don't think that's it. You're crying because you're sad. Why are you sad?'

'I just want to roost!' he blurted. 'I'm a rooster, I roost!'

'This must all be very disconcerting for you,' Azrael said, half sympathetically, half like a scientist inspecting a specimen.

'I had a simple life, Azrael. Eat, sleep, bump uglies with lady chickens, repeat. My real name isn't even Simon. They just started calling me that when they turned me into this fleshy thing with disconcertingly dangly bits!'

'What's your real name?'

'It would be unpronounceable to you.'

'Let me have a crack.'

'It's something like Buckbuckbuck Buckaw.'

'I see. Well… can we go with Bucky?'

He nodded meekly as she continued: 'What I'm hearing is that you don't actually want this job?'

'No I don't! I'm a chicken. I don't want to wear clothes and ride a motorcycle!'

'Well, why don't you just pack it in, then?'

'I can't do that,' he sighed. 'I'm a bird of my word. All those dead people out there need me.'

Overcome with misery, he slumped into an office chair, sobbing uncontrollably.

Azrael sipped her coffee thoughtfully: 'Buckle up, Bucky - I think I have a plan.'

Guthrie's wing feathers flapped in the wind, like socks on a washing line, as she flew over the dark expanse of the Atlantic Ocean.

Max could almost smell home in the air as the first distant twinkle of the coast appeared on the horizon. She felt herself getting closer to her body. Cocooned under Guthrie's thick feathers, she leaned into Graham huddled next to her.

'So what happens next?' she asked.

'If I want the job back I'm going to have to fight for it,' he replied. 'It's the only way to show I've really changed. I'll have to intercept this Simon fellow. Oh, and get you back to your body, of course.'

'But I want to help you, Graham.'

'You've already been away from your body for far too long. If we find it, you're going back in it.'

'Bu-'

'End of discussion!'

The next few minutes passed in silence with both of them considering their predicaments.

Suddenly, the sound of Guthrie's voice floated back to them on the air: 'We've got a problem!'

Her eyes were fixed on the airfield rapidly approaching. Searchlights were probing the dark clouds for signs of her. Outside the hangar was the unmistakable form of Azrael – red trench coat flapping in the wind.

'It's okay,' sighed Graham. 'I actually need a word with Azrael.'

'But you're riding in on stolen company property,' Guthrie replied. 'She'll turn you in.'

'I'm just borrowing office supplies.'

'I'm not a set a paperclips!'

'I think we can trust her. We'll just have to take the risk.'

Azrael didn't even twitch as the vast bird swooped down, obliterating the moonlight, and landed with a downdraft so powerful it knocked the searchlights off their axes.

'Hello Guthrie!' she shouted, bending her head and bowing in respect. 'Out for a midnight stroll, were you?'

Graham and Max slid down the steep hill of Guthrie's wing and landed unceremoniously on the tarmac. Graham picked himself up quickly, brushing his trousers and struggling to regain composure.

'Azrael-'

'I'm sure you've guessed they told me to bring you in as soon as your feet touched soil,' she said blankly. 'Preferably even sooner.'

A moment of terrible tension hung in the air.

'Are you going to?' Graham winced.

'Well, it's a terribly foggy night, isn't it?' Azrael smiled. 'Perhaps I lost sight of you.'

Graham, Max, and Guthrie all gave a united sigh of relief.

'I was right, by the way,' Graham said. 'Sybil architected this whole thing. Apparently, I'd become a massive arse.'

'Did she use those exact words?'

'You know Sybil. She didn't have to.'

'It's a shame you couldn't have just listened to me when I told you that,' Azrael said.

'I'm sorry.'

'This is Max, I take it?'

Graham beckoned for her to come closer: 'Yes, this is Max Godwin and she is *not* dead.'

'Congratulations,' Azrael smirked.

'It feels pretty great,' Max said and the two of them shook hands.

Azrael turned to Graham. 'Do you have a plan?'

'If I go straight back to HQ they'll arrest me before I can even plead my case. So I'll have to prove I can do the job differently... better than Simon.'

'I don't think Simon will be too much of a problem, actually,' Azrael said. 'He's having a bit of a crisis of confidence. It turns out chickens are ill-prepared to confront the gaping maw of mortality.'

'Go figure.'

'In the meantime, I've told him to start slipping up a bit. He'll do anything to avoid shouldering the responsibility anymore.'

'Excellent. Can you get me near him?'

'Sure, but you'll need your van. She's at the ferry pound and she's been pining for you. I can drop you there, but then I really have to get back.'

By the time they reached the car pound, heavy clouds had rolled in accompanied by driving rain. There wasn't a trace of light except for a string of lamps hanging from a shed at the rear of the crowded forecourt. All they could discern were rows of indistinguishable vehicles, with drops of rain plinking off wing mirrors and windshields. It felt like a graveyard of broken toys.

Shivering, they pressed their noses up against the bars of the entrance gate.

'I can't see her,' said Max.

Graham rummaged in his pocket for a set of keys. He reached between the bars and pushed the button on top.

Two orange lights flashed excitedly from the far left of the yard.

'Aha!' Graham said. 'Hello, beautiful!'

'That's great,' Max said. 'But how do we get in?'

Graham sucked his teeth: 'Doesn't seem to be anyone around. Gate's locked. Hop the fence?'

'I don't like the sound of that question mark. Don't bring me in on this decision.'

He grinned: 'Hop the fence!'

The cold wire felt smooth and slippery in their fingers as they crawled their way up and over until finally, their feet slapped down forcefully on the muddy ground on the other side.

'Are you absolutely sure there wasn't a doorbell?' Max whispered.

'Oh, yeah, I find there are always cute little doorbells attached to the fences of imposing scrapyards,' Graham replied.

He tiptoed away through the yard, his feet gently tapping in muddy puddles. Max crossed her arms and watched him. Her attention was drawn towards a shed at the back of the yard and the string of six lights hovering in front of it.

They looked like they must be on a string of some sort, but they were moving up and down now. She could have put it down to the wind, but it was not a windy night.

When Graham was within touching distance of his beloved van, he darted forward and threw his arms around the bonnet as if embracing an old friend.

'I missed you,' he sighed and the suspension groaned in response.

Max, still watching the lights, appeared by his side. 'This is all very touching, but I think we better leave.'

'What's the rush?' Graham asked, squeezing the van a bit tighter and tickling a headlight.

'I'm starting to get a bad feeling.'

Max watched with confusion and growing concern as the lights simultaneously lifted about six feet into the air.

'Uh, Graham?'

'Yeah, just give me a second to check for dings…'

Max peered through the gloom. The lights bobbed up and down and then they started getting bigger. All of a sudden, she realised they were coming closer. That's when they began to growl.

'Graham, I think the lights are angry with us.'

'What are you talking about?'

She pointed at the lanterns, now only a stone's throw away, and hollered: 'The lights are angry!'

Graham looked up and his eyes widened. He frantically searched for the phone in his pocket and flicked on the torch, sweeping the light slowly across the ground. He came to an abrupt halt when he discovered four paws the size of dinner plates, sinewy legs, a heaving barrelled chest, three necks, three snarling mouths full of bared teeth, and finally, six glowing eyes.

Max screamed and the strange beast stiffened at the noise. In one horrifying moment, it was bounding forward toward her, its mouth frothing.

Max squealed, turned and skidded away in the mud: 'Bad dog, bad dog!'

Graham ran to the back of the van and lifted the boot door open. Max leapt to get inside, her fingers slipping on the boot floor, but the dog had gained too much ground. She felt its hot breath on her skin and a sharp pain as it wrapped one of its three sets of teeth around her ankle. She cried out and tried to pull herself further into the van.

Graham pounced on the creature's muscular, coarsely-furred back, and it let go of Max in surprise.

'Get in the van,' he shouted to Max as the dog shook him left and right.

At last, Max was finally able to scramble inside. She lunged over the van's back seat, desperately rifling around for anything to help. All she found was a football, a picnic blanket, and a black cape. Her hand touched a wooden broom handle and she tried to pull it out, but it was stuck. She pulled harder and the handle suddenly freed itself, sending her spinning backwards. She realised, as she heard the sound of sharp metal ripping upholstery, that the handle was attached to a huge curved blade – a scythe.

'Here,' she yelled at Graham as she threw it roughly on the ground beside him. He was on the floor now with the slathering hound snapping at his throat.

'Thanks,' Graham croaked, with a glob of dog spit dangling millimetres from his eye. After a few attempts, he finally managed to grab the scythe's handle and held it between himself and the dog, pushing up hard to separate them.

Just when he thought he couldn't hold the powerful animal back any longer, a shrill, sharp whistle pierced the darkness and the van was instantly bathed in bright white light. The dog drew back and sat down on Graham's chest with a thud, panting from the fight.

From inside the van, Max could now see the car pound clearly. All kinds of fantastical vehicles were parked in rows - winged cars, broomsticks, a coach made out of a giant pumpkin and, in the far distance, a red and white sleigh. She felt something touch her hand and realised she was sharing the boot with a worrying number of ants.

A woman in a hooded cloak approached Graham.

'Graham?' she said with surprise.

'Euryale!' he wheezed.

'What on earth are you doing here?'

'If you could kindly call your mutt off me, I'll be happy to explain.'

'Heel,' she shouted and the great dog bounded to her side and licked her hand with all three tongues.

Hiss

'I didn't realise this was *your* yard,' Graham blustered, trying in vain to brush the muddy paw prints off his jacket as he got to his feet.

'Clearly not, or you wouldn't have thought breaking in was a smart idea!'

Max watched as Graham explained their story. Then the two of them began walking towards the van. Graham opened the boot. Max's adrenalin was wearing off and her ankle was beginning to throb.

'Good news,' Graham said. 'This lady is Euryale and she's going to help us.'

'Did you know your boot is full of ants?' Max asked.

Hiss

'Pleasure to meet you, Max,' Euryale chuckled, stretching out a hand. 'You've probably heard of my sister, Medusa.'

'As in, *the* Medusa. Monstrous gorgon lady?' Max said, limping out of the van.

'Well that's what they'd like you to think.'

'What do you mean?'

Graham cut in: 'Euryale's going to take care of you while I find Simon. She's immortal so she'll make a fine guardian.'

'Oh no, Graham!' Max said. 'I told you I was coming with you!'

'Yeah, well that bite on your leg says otherwise. It needs dressing.'

'I can walk!' Max said, wincing in pain. 'What about leaving me on my own? Drifting away and so forth.'

'I told you. You're not on your own. Euryale's here.'

Euryale shifted her position and the searchlight dimmed: 'C'mon, kid. Let's get you sorted.'

The three-headed dog whimpered an apology.

'Mm, okay,' Max said, noticing Euryale's hood undulating curiously.

Euryale sniggered: 'Don't worry, you're alright. I'm not going to turn you to stone or anything.'

'Yeah, I bet that's what your sister said right before she turned people into garden ornaments.' Max said.

'You're funny. I like you!' Euryale snorted and pulled down her hood. Max let out a yelp.

'Oh,' Euryale smiled apologetically. 'I do have snakes for hair, though.'

CHAPTER THIRTEEN

DROP DEAD

People always said that Enid Michaels would do just about anything to get out of hosting a party. They never expected that to include dying just short of her hundredth birthday.

She chuckled to herself as she sat back in her favourite armchair and waited for salvation. She was hoping they would use that joke at her funeral.

Many miles away, Graham turned the van engine on and leaned out the window.

'I won't be long,' he said to Max. 'Make sure Euryale takes a look at that ankle, please.'

'Just be careful out there, you're a marked… man?'

'Close enough.'

The van purred through the gate and Graham settled in the driver's seat: 'Back in the saddle, old girl.'

He pushed the little silver knob on the dashboard and felt the yard, the hedgerow, and the road fall far away and disappear behind him. The countryside flashed by in a second. Lanes turned to village streets to city avenues. The stars in the night sky blurred into streams of light, then the van slowed and the streams shifted back into pinpricks.

He had arrived on a street in Manchester. All around were the sounds of the city - a wailing ambulance siren, a taxicab idling, a motorbike ripping off into the distance.

Terraced, red brick houses hemmed him in. Some still had the unmistakable blue glow of a television flashing in their front window while others were in complete darkness.

'Number six,' he said, being extra sure to check his tablet, and made his way up the path. He rummaged in his trouser pocket and pulled out a door key with a skull at the top of it. The metal shifted shape in his hands, the teeth of the key going up and down. When it stabilised, Graham pushed it into the lock and felt the satisfying click as it turned with ease. Inside the house, there was a special kind of sacred stillness. He padded up the carpeted stairs, searching for a soul. He checked the tablet for the second time.

'Enid Michaels, ninety-nine, heart failure,' he said.

There was no sign of Enid. Graham's phone started vibrating in his pocket. He ignored it, pushed open a door and found himself in the master bedroom. The bed was neatly made, but various cardboard boxes were sat opened and spread across the floor, half-filled with porcelain ornaments, lamps and knick-knacks. Graham peered into a box and pulled out a bone-china spaniel. He stared intensely into its eyes.

'Where's your mistress?' he whispered to it.

'There you are,' Enid's spirit screeched from an armchair in the corner. A raven sat loftily on the chair back. Graham was so shocked he staggered backwards, nearly dropping the ornament.

'Good grief!' he shouted.

'Nearly three days I've been waiting for you,' Enid continued. 'I've watched my body getting wheeled away and all my things shoved in boxes or binned! I should be playing boules with Elvis by now.'

'You know, that's not actually the way it works, Enid.'

'That's Miss Michaels to you, young man.'

'Miss Michaels…'

'This is not the kind of shoddy service I was led to expect in The Great Beyond.'

The raven took off from the chair and flew past Graham's ear. 'She's all yours,' it croaked before disappearing down the stairs.

'I apologise for the wait E…Miss Michaels.' Graham said. 'It's been a crazy couple of days, but we're ready now. In fact, I'm actually quite short on time.'

'Trying to rush me out now, are you? Now you've taken your sweet time getting here, you want to hurry me out the door. Well I'll take my time, thank you!'

She shuffled past Graham, throwing a sharp elbow, and headed slowly down the stairs.

'...Do you want that spaniel?' she barked as Graham realised he was still holding it. 'He's Spode. I don't want my niece getting him. He'll be smithereens by Sunday week.'

Graham herded Enid down the stairs and out into the cold night air, in much the same way one might direct a nervous peacock.

'Is this it, is it?' Enid said, looking the campervan up and down. 'I never did like camping.'

Graham was about to open his mouth, but his train of thought was derailed by the approach of a motorbike. He was about to continue, but the rider seemed to be waving at him.

'Graham?' he said, as he flipped the visor up on his helmet.

'Can I help you?' Graham asked.

'Oh, bless my feathers! It is you!'

'Hey, nugget!' Graham said. 'Just the bird I was hoping to see.'

'Evening Miss Michaels,' Simon said, waving politely at the old woman as he propped the bike on its stand. 'I won't be a minute. Just have a brief conference with my colleague, here.'

'Ah, no listen. About that,' Graham said. 'I need you to let me take this one.'

'Oh, nothing would give me more pleasure.'

'Great. I'd hoped you would say that.'

'But...'

'But? No. No buts.'

'I've been thinking and, as much as I hate this job, I do have a duty of care. How do I know you'll look after all these people properly?'

'Excuse me?'

'Well, the whole reason I'm here is because you weren't doing a good job. So, I can't just hand the reins back over without some assurances, targets and peer-to-peer reviews.'

'Assurances? Listen Kentucky, you've been at this job five minutes!'

Simon swung a leather-clad leg, dismounted the bike and tucked the helmet under one arm.

'A pleasure to meet you, madam,' he bowed to Enid. 'I'm so very sorry for your loss... of yourself.'

'Oh goodness,' she swooned.

Graham rolled his eyes: 'Don't be fooled, miss. This man is a cock.'

'Language!' Enid said.

'No, he's a chicken man. Don't you see?'

'I don't think I do,' she puffed. 'This nice young hunk is going to let me ride on the back of his motorbike.'

Simon nodded with an expression of deepest, earnest sorrow etched on his features. He turned his attention back to Graham: 'Just go back to HQ, plead your case and ask for your job back. That way I can go back to my lovely little farm and try to forget all the incredibly traumatising things I've seen.'

'I can't do that, Simon,' Graham said. 'The board want me arrested. That's why I need you to start doing a bad job, so I can swoop in and save the day. Understand?'

'Well that cooks your goose,' Simon said as he sat on the motorbike and put his helmet back on. 'I won't compromise my standards and I can't possibly hand the job over to a wanted felon!'

'Oh, a criminal,' Enid said as she perched side-saddle on the pillion and grabbed hold of Simon's waist. 'Step on it, Simon.'

'Hang on!' Graham shouted over the revving of the bike.

Simon looked him square in the eyes. 'Hand yourself in, Graham. It's the only way.'

He flipped down his visor and zoomed off into the distance. Enid's squeals of delight echoed along the quiet street.

'Right, fine, okay,' Graham blustered, throwing his hands in the air. 'So it's like that then, is it? Let's see how fast you can really go on that hunk of junk.'

He jumped back in the driver's seat of the van and headed to the next soul on the list and the next and the next. Every time Simon was there to greet him, grimacing apologetically before speeding off into the distance.

Max had watched Graham's van disappear all the way around the bend before she limped over to Euryale's hut. The interior was a shrine to wood panelling. A faded photo of a sunflower hung on a lonely nail on the back wall. There was a very small kitchen in one corner, a desk of some sort in the other, and a squashed sofa between the two. Max sat on a plastic chair as the gorgon rifled in a filing cabinet for a first aid kit.

'How is this even possible?' Max said, staring at her bleeding ankle.

'Well,' said Euryale with a safety pin between her teeth. 'It's a good sign, really.'

'I can't wait to hear this.'

'It means you still have a tie to your physical body,' Euryale said, dabbing at the wound with some antiseptic. 'Ah, you see, this isn't half as bad as it looks.'

'Spoken like a woman trying to avoid a lawsuit.'

Euryale chuckled. The dog plodded in and slid its three heads gently onto Max's knee before she could back away. She felt his warm drool soak through her trousers.

'That means he's sorry,' Euryale said. 'He was just protecting his mistress.'

'Oh,' Max said nervously while stroking one of his ears like he was a lion with a nuclear warhead in his jaws. 'What's his name?'

'Um, he has many names.'

'I only need one.'

'Just call him anything, it's fine.'

'Well, you have to tell me what his name is now!'

'It's just a bit embarrassing. In ancient languages he sounded so cool, but two thousand years later here we still are. In your tongue his name sort of sounds a lot like...'

'Yes?'

'Kippers.'

Graham sat in his van, now parked outside the Easy Slumber Hotel. "Hand yourself in,' he harrumphed. 'What a bone-headed arse. Holier-than-thou, feather-brained eejit.'

He picked at the skin on his fingers.

'Simon Coe-Pomp. Simon Coe-Pompous, more like.'

The sound of a motorbike purring through the docks drifted on the still night air. It grew louder and louder until the bike appeared from behind a building. Simon flipped up his helmet's visor and brought the bike to stop outside the hotel door. His passenger dismounted - a younger man, maybe twenty years old.

'I'm so sorry,' Simon sniffed. 'Have a good one.'

The man nodded, then headed inside with a look of utter bewilderment.

Graham tutted and leapt out of the van, pointing a finger at Simon. 'Hold it right there, fillet!'

'I've told you already, Graham. If you're on the run I have nothing to say to you.'

'Who made you the boss of who gets this job and who doesn't?'

'Unlike you, I take this job very seriously! It needs an even hand on the tiller. Even if I did want to hand everything over, you're a wanted being. They'll arrest you as soon as you get back here with a soul and probably turn me into roast dinner for helping you!'

Simon could still recall the house in Liverpool he had visited the day before. An older couple had been in the middle of lunch and invited him to join. When they asked him to carve the chicken he hadn't stopped screaming for twenty minutes. What a day that had been.

Simon shuddered and began preparing to leave as Graham's thoughts raced frantically.

'Uh, wait, Simon!'

'Hmm?'

'Listen, before you go, I'm starving, do you fancy a snack? It's a long day of riding ahead for you on that thing.'

'I really don't think that's appropriate, Graham. Do you?'

'Ah, you're probably right,' Graham said, scratching his head in defeat. 'I'll just eat this popcorn all by myself.'

Simon stopped adjusting the bike and removed his helmet: 'Did you say corn?'

'Oh, yeah, popped corn. Popcorn.'

Simon's stomach rumbled. He gulped and got off the bike: 'I guess a beak-full wouldn't hurt.'

Graham grinned: 'I'll get the bag out of the van.'

He reached into the glove box and pulled out the popcorn. Slowly, he opened the bag, took out a piece and held it out for Simon to take. At the last second he dropped it on the ground.

'Ah, gosh. I'm sorry. Butter fingers!'

'No matter,' said Simon, drooling. 'I prefer to eat from the ground.' In a flash he had bent down and eaten the popcorn.

Graham took a step backwards, now only a foot away from the van. He repeated the process, dropping another piece, apologising and allowing Simon to eat it off the floor.

'Do you know what?' he said, before the third attempt. 'Why don't we just eat in the van?'

Graham pretended to trip, threw the bag through the van's open passenger door and onto the backseat, sending popcorn flying in all directions.

'Oh no!' Simon said, diving in after it without thinking. He began shovelling handfuls into his mouth. Graham slammed the van door behind him and locked it.

'Just a minute!' Simon shouted as Graham got in the driver's seat. 'What are you doing?'

'I'm kidnapping you, I guess!'

Simon lunged forward, but Graham had already started the engine and pushed the little silver button.

'Seatbelts, please,' he said as the force of acceleration sent Simon hurtling backwards, gripped to the backseat.

Shakily, he pulled the belt across his chest: 'Cluck.'

It was still raining at the garage. Puddles joined with other puddles until they formed giant muddy lakes across the yard. The water was cleaning the dust off every vehicle, only to leave it dirtier than before.

'What did you mean about your sister?' Max winced as she lifted her dressed leg onto the sofa. Kippers was snoring softly in front of her – each head taking it in turns to breathe in and out.

Snort, snort, snort.
Whistle, whistle, whistle.

Euryale shifted in her chair and sipped a cup of steaming tea. 'It's a sad story.'

'I've been hanging around with Graham, I'm used to those.'

'Okay. Medusa was my mortal sister. You remind me of her, actually. She was funny too and independent. We were very close, like best friends as well as family.'

'Wait, I thought she was a monster?'

'History has written her differently.'

'What happened to her?'

'The real monster showed up. A man. He did things to her. Things she didn't want him to do.'

Euryale's snakes began to writhe and hiss. Max stared into her eyes as she took a deep breath and continued.

'This guy's wife blamed Medusa for her husband's infidelity,' she continued. 'She cursed my sister so she could never look at another man or woman again. I could never see her. She couldn't even look in a mirror. They called her a beast.'

'I'm so sorry,' said Max.

'Mm, it gets worse.'

'She was killed, right?'

'A few years later, yes. Perseus, big, brave, hard man that he was, killed her in her sleep. They called him a hero for it. He took her head as a trophy. How sick is that?'

'Blimey Euryale, I don't know what to say…'

'I told you it was sad.'

'Doesn't it make you angry?'

'Of course, but what am I going to do about it now, kiddo? Other than telling her story.'

Euryale took a ring from her pocket, a curling golden serpent with green emerald eyes. 'This was hers. You should have it.'

'Are you sure?' Max asked, her voice quivering as she took the ring and admired it. 'It's beautiful,' she said, stifling a yawn.

'You need some sleep, it's late,' Euryale said checking the clock on the wall. 'Actually, it's early!'

She reached up, pulled a soft blanket from above the sofa, and laid it gently over Max as she yawned again.

'There's just no way I can get to sleep,' Max said, lying down resting her head on a cushion.

'Well just think quiet thoughts until breakfast time then,' Euryale said, turning down the lights. Opening the door, she looked back at Max and saw she was already fast asleep.

At that moment, Graham's campervan skidded round the corner into the muddy yard.

Euryale quietly clicked the shed door shut and quickly made her way over.

She could hear muffled cries of indignation coming from inside the van.

Graham hopped out in a hurry before the wheels had even stopped rolling. 'Where's Max?'

'She's sleeping. Who's that?' she said, pointing at Simon, who was now banging on the window of the van and shouting for help.

'He's the chicken the board of directors replaced me with,' Graham said.

'You kidnapped him?'

'You know what, I didn't have a lot of choice. Can you believe he wouldn't let me do the job?'

'It's not totally beyond the realms of understanding.'

'Not you as well? Listen I'm good at this job. I want this job. I care about this job! Why does no one believe me?'

'I guess people want to see some proof.'

'Well, they aren't going to get any unless they let me try, are they?'

Euryale shrugged and they suddenly realised that Simon had stopped shouting. As they turned to check on him, the van began to roll forwards.

Euryale said: 'I don't suppose there's any chance you left the hand brake off, is there?'

Graham broke into a run, but the van engine had already turned on. Simon sat up in the driver's seat, where he had been hunched down, and gave a jaunty little wave.

Death may come on swift wings, but he runs on human feet. Graham was only just able to put a solitary finger on the van's door handle before Simon found the silver button and immediately streaked out of view.

'Great!' Graham said. 'Now he's got my van and my job!'

'Where do you think he's headed?' Euryale asked, running up behind him.

'Bet you anything he's going back to HQ to rat me out.'

'He's been through a lot, Graham. I think he's done a pretty good job considering he was pecking corn last week. I think it's quite sweet that he cares so much about a job he's been forced to do.'

'I care!'

'Well, you certainly do now.'

'If I chase Simon to HQ I'm absolutely getting arrested. You know that, right?'

'Maybe that's what it will take. Perhaps you're going to have to risk that to make the board see how much you want this job. I reckon they'll at least let you speak to them. You were born to be Death, Graham. It's who you are.'

Graham stood in silence for a moment, rubbing his hands together to fight the cold.

'When did you get so wise?' he finally sniffed.

'I'm over two thousand years old.'

'Two thousand? You're just a baby!'

'Well, I do know a few things.'

'Do you know how I can get to Swindon?'

'I have an idea.'

CHAPTER FOURTEEN

ON A ONE-HORSE OPEN SLAY

Graham stared dumbfounded at the broomstick hovering in front of him. Euryale had been searching deep in the rows of parked vehicles before skimming it across the ground at Graham's feet.

'It's not that bad,' Euryale said, approaching and witnessing the sneer creeping over Graham's face.

'Don't you have anything with doors? Or a seat belt?'

'There's the pumpkin, but it won't get you to Swindon before next week.'

'What about that?' Graham said, pointing to the red and white sleigh at the back.

Euryale sucked air through her teeth: 'I'm not taking you to Swindon in that, Graham. The big man is expecting her back at the Pole quite soon.'

'Oh, so it's *the* sleigh, is it? Doesn't look like much.'

'Are you kidding?' Euryale shrieked and dragged Graham towards the shimmering carriage. 'Nine reindeer-power engine, hand-woven red leather upholstery, walnut dashboard, state-of-the-art GPS, climate control, vermillion and cream custom paint job. Only driven by a little old man once a year.'

'How fast does she go?'

Euryale stroked the sleigh's bonnet: 'Relatively fast.'

'Can you be more specific?'

'No, I am being specific. It travels using relativity. Five hours in this baby could be five minutes in real time.

'Are you saying I could travel to HQ in seconds?'

'Precisely.'

'Why don't I have this technology?'

'Well, your van works by using materialisation - meaning you arrive just after a person has died. In this, you'd be travelling so quick you could be there before they died.'

Graham's eyes widened: 'Awesome.'

'Nope, not doing it. I don't know if you've ever met Saint Nick, but he's not to be trifled with. I don't want to end up on the naughty list.'

'Don't you think helping a friend in need is precisely the sort of thing that gets you on the nice list?'

'Ah...' Euryale scratched her head aggressively as Graham did his best to look cute and vulnerable. 'I'm going to get in such trouble for this!'

'Almost certainly!'

'But we need a reindeer.'

'Isn't there anything else we can use?'

Euryale mused for a moment, before exclaiming: 'Kippers!'

The hound came bounding over at the sound of his name and Graham yelped.

'C'mon Graham, he's a powerful dog - he can do it. Unless you want to stick yourself in the harness?'

Graham looked suspiciously at Kippers and the dog barked excitedly.

'Yeah, he's powerful alright. He could rip your head off, spit in it, and still have a mouth spare to lick his....'

'Graham,' interrupted Euryale. 'Be a man, and get in the pretty sleigh.'

She attached Kippers to the front of the vehicle as Graham hopped in and started fiddling with the dashboard.

'Very nice, very classy,' he cooed. 'Walnut, you say?'

'Get your mucky paws off!'

Euryale gave Kippers a reassuring pat and climbed aboard next to Graham: 'Right, off we go then. Budge up, I'm driving.'

'Righto.'

'Wait! What about Max?'

Graham winced: 'She can't come with us. It's not safe.'

'Well, she can't stay here.'

'You said this sleigh works relatively, right?'

'Right. Where are you going with this?'

'So, we could be back here again before we even leave.'

'I guess?'

'You guess or you know?'

'I know.'

'I'll hold you to that.'

Euryale punched a button on the dashboard and Kippers took off from the ground with the ease of someone pushing off from the bottom of a swimming pool. He tugged the sleigh into the air and Graham watched with curiosity as the world below appeared to slow down. A car on a country lane crawled at a snail's pace. The clouds in the sky skidded to a halt. The trees stopped swaying in the breeze.

Graham grinned: 'Ho, ho, h...'

'Don't you dare,' Euryale interjected, covering his mouth with a gloved hand.

As the sleigh descended, time appeared to return to its normal pace again. The yellow bloom of dawn was appearing just behind Swindon hospital. Graham spied his campervan parked in a disabled space near the entrance.

'Would you mind taking that back with you?' he said, gesturing to the van.

'I'll just shove it in the boot, shall I?' Euryale said.

'Can't you tow it?'

'No! Santa's sleigh doesn't tow!'

'Fine!' he said, clambering down onto the pavement. 'Wish me luck!'

Euryale held his gaze for a moment. 'You've got this, okay?'

He took a deep breath. 'Thank you.'

A cold blast of air-conditioning hit him in the face as he stepped inside the hospital and made his way to the stairwell. Todd the porter, at the reception desk, leapt to his feet and frantically pushed a panic button until his knuckle seized up.

'Chill out, Todd,' breezed Graham, as sirens blared and lights flashed all around him.

When he finally reached the door to the thirteenth floor, four burly guards were waiting.

'Ah,' he puffed as they stepped forwards. 'That won't be necessary, chaps. I've come to explain this whole blasted mess.'

'Mr Reaper, we're detaining you for the unlawful capture of an Apoco employee, impersonating an Apoco employee, and misuse of Apoco property.'

'Now, now, gentlemen,' Graham said, standing as tall as he possibly could. 'Does that sound like something I would do?'

The guards looked at each other for a second.

'Do you really think that I, of all people, have the time to go swanning about taking hostages? Stealing things? Death - a petty thief?'

'It does sound unlikely, sir.'

'Well, don't you think it's worth double checking before you go infringing on my rights? You really, really don't want to get on the wrong side of me.'

The guards turned towards each other to consult on this unexpected turn of events.

'Okay, Mr Reaper,' one guard announced, turning around to find Graham on the other side of the glass panel of the door to floor thirteen. He rushed to push it open, but it had been jammed from the other side.

Graham waved at the perplexed guard: 'Terribly sorry.'

He then raced out of view and off down the long corridor, shoes squeaking on the vinyl.

'Azrael!' he bellowed as he burst through her office door, only to find himself face-to-knee with Simon Coe-Pomp, perched like a tropical bird on an office chair.

'Oh,' Graham said, not missing a beat. 'I see Nincompoop's beaten me here. You back-stabbing little fillet.'

'You know very well that's not my name.'

'But of course you got here before I did. You were driving my van.'

'You mean the one you kidnapped me in? Yes, yes I did.'

'I had to, didn't I? If you'd just stepped aside all of this would be sorted by now!'

'Children, children,' Azrael shouted from across the room, snapping both of them to attention. 'Don't make me bang your heads together.'

'He started it,' Simon said, looking at the carpet.

'That's true,' Azrael replied. 'None of this is your fault, Simon. But, if you'd handed control back over to Graham, like I very nicely asked you to, we might've had a shot at fixing this.'

Graham smiled smugly and rubbed his hands together, before Azrael rounded on him too.

'And I don't know what you're smirking about,' she said. 'Kidnapping Buckbuckbuck-'

Graham blinked: 'I'm sorry? Buckbuckbuck?'

'Yes, that's Simon's real name. Kidnapping him was absolutely the wrong call. How can I protect you now without endangering myself, Graham? You're a fugitive.'

'If I could just talk to the board, I can show them how much I want this job,' Graham said desperately. 'How much I've changed.'

From down the hall came the sound of pounding boots.

'Graham,' Azrael said. 'Were it not for Simon, there would be more souls on Earth than living people right now. Ghost sightings went up two thousand per cent. How we haven't mislaid anyone else is a minor miracle. Every raven in the country is out looking after these poor people. We were even forced to bring in some foreign ravens. As usual, Muggins here has been left to pick up the pieces!'

There was a knock on the door. The four guards Graham had previously evaded marched in without waiting for an answer.

'How about we try this again, Mr Reaper,' one of them said.

'We're also adding endangerment of life to your offences, Mr Reaper,' another added.

'Eh, where did you get that from?'

'You blocked a fire escape. We had to force the door open. If an evacuation of the floor had been required, everyone in here would have perished.'

'Oh, come on! Half the people on this floor are already dead!'

'Also, your van was parked in a disabled space,' a smaller guard grumbled through a thick moustache.

'I wasn't the one that parked it! Azrael, this is madness!!'

'Guys, guys, are all these charges really necessary?' Azrael said, as the guards cuffed Graham and led him to the door. 'It seems a little heavy-handed.'

One glared at her: 'Would you like us to arrest you for aiding and abetting, ma'am?'

'Uh, no. No, thank you. Don't worry, Graham. I'm sure we can straighten all this out somehow.'

Graham lowered his head as he crossed the threshold and began walking down the corridor with his elbows held by the two tallest guards.

'What a silly boy, you've been,' said moustache man, this time in a more familiar voice. 'Not your day, is it?'

He raised his hat slightly to reveal a shock of pink hair. Graham's jaw dropped.

'Not a word from you, sonny, continued Sybil, lowering her hat. We're going to be on the road for a bit. Do you need a toilet break of any kind before we leave?'

'Is that really necessary?' another guard groaned.

'Do you want urine all over the back of the van?' Sybil said. 'I can tell you from experience, it is not pleasant. And the smell…'

She walked up to Graham and unlocked his cuffs. 'He can't very well take a whizz with his hands in irons, can he?' she said.

Graham looked at Sybil and she winked.

'Take care of Max,' he whispered.

Sybil arched an eyebrow meaningfully, ripped off the fake moustache and smiled: 'Run.'

CHAPTER FIFTEEN

A MATTER OF LIFE AND DEATH

A javelin of early morning sun pierced Max's eyelids as Euryale clinked mugs into the sink on the other side of the scrapyard shed.

'Umpf,' Max said.

'Morning, beautiful! Did I wake you? Sorry.'

'S'okay.'

'Probably just as well. It's getting on for 6am, you know.'

Max had dreamt she had faded away, floating on the wind like a fallen leaf. Then there had been the sound of sleigh bells for some reason. She could not shake the feeling of a lucky escape.

Kippers padded in and licked Max's hand affectionately.

'How long have you been up?' Max asked Euryale.

'Oh, I haven't slept,' she replied, turning around and grinning with the slight twinkle of mania in her eyes. 'Sleep is for wimps.'

Max felt suddenly on the alert: 'Did Graham come back?'

'Yes, but things got a bit complicated.'

'That sounds ominous.'

Euryale took a deep breath: 'Graham kidnapped his replacement.'

'Simon the chicken man?'

'Exactly so. Then Simon stole Graham's van and ran off to Apoco HQ in Swindon. Graham asked me to take him up there, so I gave him a lift in Santa's sleigh.'

Max sat motionless as the many thoughts in her head rolled up their sleeves and started landing blows on each other.

Euryale continued: 'And then I got back here just in time because you seemed to be turning a little bit... transparent in your sleep. Not to worry though, all fixed now.'

'Why did you leave me here alone?'

'I wanted to bring you, but Graham said it was too dangerous.'

'Why?'

'Well, there's a good chance he's going to be arrested.'

'Arrested? What happens if he's arrested?'

'You know, I'm not really sure. I guess he goes to some kind of purgatorial jail? I'm sure he got there in time and managed to plead his case, though.'

'Wouldn't he be back by now.'

Euryale checked the clock on the wall: 'Mm, yeah. Good point.'

'What's the quickest way to Swindon?'

Euryale rolled her eyes: 'Santa is going to have my head on a candy cane.'

'So why Swindon?' Max asked, hobbling across the freshly rained-upon car park of Apoco HQ.

'You're kidding, right?' Euryale laughed as she tied Kippers' reins to a bike rack, then used her sleeve to polish away a smudge on the sleigh's paintwork. 'Ever heard of the Magic Roundabout? Five mini roundabouts in a circle?'

Max looked at her blankly.

'It's an utterly pointless traffic measure, but it makes an excellent rune of protection,' Euryale continued. 'We don't even have to go out there and redraw it – every car, truck and moped does that for us every day.' She started cackling: 'Five mini roundabouts in a circle. Five!'

Max and Euryale stepped through the hospital's entrance doors. There was a chill in the air and the main hall seemed to stretch on forever, filled with people in varying states of distress. The various pieces of lifeless, utilitarian furniture looked as if they had conspired to quietly disintegrate together and wait to see if anyone noticed. No one had.

'Don't sit down,' Euryale whispered with a hint of urgency. 'The chairs will drain your soul.'

Beep!

'What was that?' Max asked. The noise was faint, but unmistakable - a blip floating on the sanitised air.

'What are you talking about?' Euryale muttered, patting her pockets down in search of a mislaid security card.

Beep! ...Beep! ...Beep!

'That!' Max said.

'We have to keep moving, pumpkin,' Euryale said, gesturing to a stairwell door with her retrieved key card in hand. 'Graham will have gone this way.'

Max stopped suddenly in her tracks. At the far end of the hall, she spotted the back of a person that looked remarkably like her mother.

Beep.

Max hovered for a second, torn between the rapidly disappearing figure and the open stairwell door. Then the woman sneezed. It made an unmistakable and instantly recognisable sound that cut through the hospital hubbub - like a terrier being launched into space.

'That's my mum,' Max said quietly.

Beep.

Euryale turned, and shifted uncomfortably from one foot to another: 'Come on, we're wasting time.'

'This is crazy, but I just saw my mum.'
'Seriously?'
'I'm sure.'
'Do you think it's possible your body is here? Death HQ of all places!'
'I know, it would be a crazy coincidence.'

Max's eyes widened as a particularly stubborn penny dropped: 'There are no coincidences. This is Sybil's doing! She knew. She knew I'd make it here.'

'Well, you have to go then. Go find your body!'

'But what about Graham?'

'I'll go to the thirteenth floor and see what's happened to him.'

'What if you need my help?'

'Don't worry - just go!'

Max hesitated for a moment, then began limping quickly down the corridor, dodging dawdling and slow-moving patients.
She squinted past the crowd to the bank of lifts and watched as her mum got in an open elevator and turned to face her. There she was. It felt as if she hadn't seen her in decades. Her warm, brown eyes looked tired and emotionless and her hair was lank and tied up scruffily. The doors slid shut and Max, heart pounding, hurriedly searched for a staircase.

Beep.

At the landing of the third floor, she poked her head into the corridor and saw her mum walking towards a ward entrance. The beeps she could hear were getting louder.

'Hello, Linda,' a passing nurse said to her mum.

Max ran to catch up and she and her mum walked side by side through the door. They went down a short corridor and into a brightly-lit room containing four beds. Her mum straightened her posture and fixed a smile, heading straight to a bay by the window. The whole room was alive with the rhythmic beeping of various life-maintaining machines.

BEEP. BEEP. BEEP.

'Hello, poppet,' her mum said to a shape lying in the bed.

Max shuddered as her eyes fell upon the figure under the covers – pale, covered in wires, a little bruised, but unmistakably herself.

'Oh,' was all Max could manage to get out of her mouth as she watched her mum sit down at her bedside.

'I tidied your room today,' her mum said. 'You're going to love what I've done with it. Even gave it a lick of paint. I only finished a couple of hours ago.' She inspected her nails, flecked with tiny dots of green - Max's favourite colour.

'This is a very sick joke, Sybil,' Max whispered as she sat down on the other side of her own body. At that moment, someone gently placed a hand on her shoulder. Max jolted forwards as though she'd been shocked. She turned around sharply to find Sybil in a nurse's uniform smiling tenderly.

'It's no joke, dearie,' she said as a doctor bustled in with a clipboard in his hand. He started talking to Max's mum, pointing animatedly at Max's ankle which was poking out of the sheets and heavily bandaged.

'A dog bite in a hospital?' Max's mum said incredulously.

'You were actually safest here,' Sybil continued. 'I diverted your ambulance just to get you in this hospital. I knew you'd come here, you see?'

'What do you mean?' Max said.
Sybil eyes twinkled. She leaned forward and whispered in her ear: 'You're going to save him. You could get back in your body right now - but you're going to save him instead.'

'I don't understand. I want to wake up. I want to go back to my normal life.'

'You gave him back his purpose.'

'I know I gave him purpose, Sybil!' Max said. 'Why does no one ever talk about me? About how I'm feeling? You threw me out in the road like a set of tyre spikes – like human bait!'

'Oh Max, give yourself more credit than that. You've taught him what it means to be mortal, to treasure your soul, to laugh. Before you, he hadn't spent more than five minutes in the company of a human being. Do you think he would have got that from just anyone?'

Max could not find the words. She looked at herself, lying in bed, looking so vulnerable. The beeps from the machine began quickening. The doctor and Max's mum broke off their conversation.

'Oh,' her mum gasped. 'Something's happening. Max are you there, can you hear me, love?'

Max took a deep breath: 'Mum?'

She watched as her body's lips began mouthing the word. Max could feel the connection getting stronger and more urgent by the minute. She knew instinctively that if she really fought right now, in this moment, her nightmare would finally come to an end.

'Wait a second,' she turned to ask Sybil. 'What do you mean "save him"?'

But Sybil was already gone. In her place, was Euryale, eyes wide with panic.

'Max!' she shrieked. 'Graham's been arrested. He's on the run!'

'Sweetheart,' her mum shrieked as the beeping began to slow again. 'Stay with me, please stay with me.'

The doctor ran from the room, calling for help, as her mum crumpled over the bed and sobbed quietly.

'Oh, Max,' Euryale said, staring at the body. 'This is you, right?'

'Yup, this is me. Not my best look, I have to say.'

'You must go then, get back to your body. I can handle Graham.'

'No. I saved him and then he saved me and now it's my turn again.'

Max hung her head low. She reached across the bed and touched her mum's hand.

'I'll be back, Mum. I have to save a friend.'

Beep.
Beep.
Beep.

CHAPTER SIXTEEN

GOING TO WAR

Graham arrived, almost without thinking, at his sister's bright red front door.

He hesitated for a moment, looking up and down the street, before knocking forcefully on the oak panels. Inside, he could hear the sound of a child screaming something about mashed potato. A woman's muffled voice replied, half amused, half exasperated. Suddenly the door swung open.

'Ha!' the woman laughed ruefully. She leaned on her doorframe and tossed a ginger plait of hair over her shoulder. Behind her, a small child launched a bowl of peas at the wall with a crash. The woman didn't blink. 'Finally remembered we exist, eh? Right as we're about to sit down to lunch.'

'Afternoon, Flannery.'

'Come in then, tosspot. Watch out for Wyatt. He left some toast around here somewhere.'

Graham stepped inside, wiped his feet on the mat and took off his boots. The little boy came streaking past him with no trousers on and marched up the stairs. He was waving an empty toilet roll tube and he had baked beans down the back of his knees.

'Ah,' Graham said with a sigh, lifting a leg and checking his sock. 'I found the toast.'

'What are you doing here, Graham?' Flannery called as she walked to the kitchen and wrenched a bed sheet from the washing machine.

'I was in the neighbourhood.'

'Were you heck! You haven't been in my neighbourhood since...'

'1916,' Graham replied bleakly as he slung the sticky, buttery toast slice in the bin.

'Oh, yeah. Busy day for you, wasn't it?'

'Hmm, I remember you standing in No Man's Land, screaming through the artillery fire.'

Flannery stopped wrestling and looked almost wistful for an instant. 'Yeah,' she grinned. 'Good times.'

'Your bloodlust is showing, Flan.'

'I'm War, what am I supposed to do?' she said, giving the sheet a final, violent tug. 'And don't call me Flan. I feel like a pudding when you do that.'

'Sorry, pudding. How is the warmongering business these days anyway?'

'Ah, it's a work-from-home job now,' Flannery said as she hung the sheet on a radiator. 'It's all drones and robots and missile tests.'

'Must be frustrating,' Graham replied.

She turned and winked: 'I do a lot of trolling on Facebook.'

As the cold afternoon air whistled past Max's ears she realised she didn't have the slightest clue where to start looking for Graham. She gazed blankly at the passing clouds, which were scudding in wisps over the bonnet of the gleaming red sleigh.

'Perhaps we should find a graveyard?' she hollered over the rush of wind.

Euryale rolled her eyes. 'Bit on the nose, isn't it?'

'Uh, some kind of mystic cupboard?'

'A cupboard?'

'To hide in!'

'He's not hiding, Max. There's nowhere he could go where he wouldn't be found. He'll be seeking counsel from someone he trusts.'

Max could feel a familiar sensation creeping back into her veins – a faintness and exhaustion she had not sensed since those few panicked hours on board the ferry to The Afterward. It had been sneaking up on her slowly, but now she felt overcome by it. She slumped in her chair.

'Are you okay?' Euryale shouted.

'I... I don't think so. Are we heading to The Afterward?'

'No, we're sort of drifting in the general direction of Manchester.'

'Then why do I feel like I'm dying?'

Max slid further in her chair, sinking into the footwell of the sleigh. Euryale looked down, her face wrought with anxiety.

'Oh no, no, no. Graham said you'd be okay with me. Max stay awake!'

'Hm...'

'I'm not strong enough to keep you safe. Graham's the only one who can keep you here now.'

Max was slipping away before Euryale's eyes.
'Where would he go? Where would I go?'
Max mumbled something unintelligible.
'What is it, pumpkin?'
Euryale bent down and put her ear to Max's mouth. She heard one single word: 'Medusa.'
'Clever girl,' Euryale said. She hurriedly punched in coordinates on the sleigh dashboard. 'Family. Yes, that's where Graham's gone. To his family.'

As the clock struck 7:30pm, silence descended upon Flannery's home. Somewhere in the darkened folds of a feather duvet, Wyatt had fallen into unconsciousness, dreaming of broadswords and pure, unfiltered rage.

Flannery handed Graham a glass of wine that was larger than his head while he reclined on her sofa. She curled up in the armchair.

'Silence at last,' she said, reaching for a copy of The Bible sitting on the shelf above.

'You gonna chapter and verse me to oblivion, are you?'

She flashed Graham a smile as she opened the book and retrieved a large bar of chocolate. She snapped it in half and tossed one part to Graham.

'So then, brother dearest,' she said, sucking loudly on her first square of chocolate. 'Is there no way to win back your title?'

'I don't know. If I could think of a way to prove myself I would. I just want to set things right, restore the balance. Everything's higgledy-piggledy.'

'Never said that word before in your life, have you?'

'Not once.'

'Why don't you send matey to The Afterward?'

'Oh, I'm sure Euryale's already helped Max back to her body. Sybil's grand plan, no doubt.'

'No, not that matey. The other matey.'

'Hmm?'

'Whatshisface. The other Max.'

'Oh,' said Graham, his eyes widening. 'Oh!' he exclaimed, this time more loudly.

'Shush, you'll wake up the warlord!'

'Flannery, you're a genius. I'll take the other Max to the ferry. He's not on any lists, so Simon can't beat me to it.'

He wriggled himself out of the sofa and into a standing position with rather less grace than he had hoped.

'I have to go,' he said, extending his arms as if to hug Flannery.

She stood and brushed the crumbs off her jumper. 'Blimey, you really are out of sorts.'

'Hush your mouth,' he said and the pair hugged.

Suddenly, there was a great rumbling from outside and then the sound of pounding footsteps up the garden path.

'They've found me, Flan,' Graham hissed.

'Quickly,' she said, tugging him towards the hallway. She flung open the cupboard under the stairs, pulled out a huge battle axe and swung it up high in readiness: 'And don't call me, Flan.'

'Shame,' Graham said, bouncing up and down on his heels. 'I would've really liked to try and put things right.'

He took a sharp breath and swiftly opened the front door. His face immediately turned from fear to concern.

'It's Max,' Euryale panted from the threshold. 'She's dying!' She stepped aside and gestured towards the upended sleigh lying sideways on the grass. Max was propped up beside it like a rag doll.

Graham ran down the path, his socks slipping on the cold, wet mud of the lawn. He felt himself scream Max's name and then he was beside her, holding her hand tightly. He noticed the translucency of her fingertips and let out an anguished cry. Anger came quickly then, like a dragon roused from its dreams.

'Why is she not back in her body?' he said. 'I trusted you to look after her!'

Euryale brushed a tear from her eye and shook her head insistently, her snakes rising up in the wind. 'It was her choice, Graham! Her body was right in front of her and she left it there for you. She said she saved you and then you saved her and now it was her turn again.'

'I don't want her to die, Euryale,' Graham said. 'We've come so far. She had so many things she wanted to do.'

They fell silent. Graham held Max's hand tightly, Flannery held Euryale's hand and above them, in the darkness of the house, Wyatt gripped hold of his favourite blanket. He pushed his nose to the window and wished for something entirely selfless for the first time in his little life.

A group of shadowy figures sat in a parked car across the road found themselves wishing too. One even reached into the infinite chasm of a suit pocket, formulated from the very fabric of the universe, and drew out a long, silvery hankie.

Graham, head bowed low to the ground, felt the smallest twitch of the hand in his.

'Graham?' Max said meekly. 'Is that really you?' He allowed himself to release a sob he had, he realised, been holding in for almost six million years.

The car across the street rolled up its window and drove silently off into the night as the strange collection of creatures, huddled on a suburban lawn, drew closer and held each other tight.

CHAPTER SEVENTEEN

THE LONG GOODBYE

A lark was twittering at the top of its lungs in a hedgerow just outside Chudleigh when the campervan rolled to a stop in front of it, ruining the performance. Typical, it thought.

Max, in the passenger seat, pulled her knees closer as Graham yanked up on the handbrake.

'I'm beginning to think I may never truly get out of this village,' she sighed.

The van whinnied back in sympathy.

'Well, I think it looks charming,' Euryale said from the backseat, as she plucked another popcorn kernel from the upholstery.

'Talk about deja vu,' Graham replied. He reached into the van's glove compartment, found a woolly hat, and slammed it shut. 'Well, if there's one place you want to find yourself stuck, a little village in Devon ain't half bad, eh?'

'Optimism from Death,' Max chuckled. 'I must have really had an effect on you, Mr Reaper!'

'You two go on without me,' Euryale said, nervously. 'I've got a very uncomfortable phone call to make with Santa Claus.'

Graham and Max headed up the road to the cottage, asphalt crunching under their feet.

'You really didn't have to come with me, you know,' Graham smiled.

'I really did,' Max replied. 'To be honest, I'm just a bit curious about the "other me."'

He stopped walking and looked Max in the eye: 'You have to stick with me though, okay? And take it easy. I can't have you going all wispy again.'

'It felt so strange,' Max said, squinting at the morning sun. 'Like I was thinning out and forgetting everything. Like I was being erased almost.'

'That's exactly what it was,' said Graham.

They started walking again – past an entrance gate and down the driveway. 'I'm a guide of sorts, I suppose. I direct all these delicate souls to a place where they can be safe, but without me they become aimless, lost. There's only so much a consciousness can take before it just drifts away. Frankly, I'm astonished we've kept you like this for so long.'

'It's only been a few days!'

'Yes, but we've packed a lot in.'

'What about this guy, then?' Max said, gesturing up the path to the house in front of them. 'How's he still here?'

'Ah,' Graham raised a finger. 'He's had company too.'

They arrived at Mallory's cottage. The front door was shut and covered with police tape.

Graham reached over and pushed the doorbell.

'What kind of company?' Max whispered.

'Positively demonic,' Graham grinned, as the door swung open.

'Morning Graham,' came a tiny, croaking voice from somewhere near the floor. Out of the shadows hopped a familiar little raven.

'Doris!' Max cried as she ran to hug the bird, picking her up and scratching her head.

'Ah, hello,' Doris replied. She perched on Max's shoulder and gave her an affectionate nip on the ear. 'Where in the blue blazes have you been?'

From down the hall, a voice with a Scottish accent floated to them. 'Doris? Who is it, lass?'

'Alright gang, this way,' Doris said, flapping off towards the voice. Max and Graham followed behind, eventually coming out of the dark hallway and into a bright and airy kitchen. Sitting at the table was a man in a dressing gown holding a cup of tea. He looked up and smiled with warm blue eyes.

'I wasn't expecting two of you,' he said. 'Work experience is it?'

'Something like that,' Graham said, sitting down awkwardly at the table. 'I'm very sorry about all this, Max.'

'Och, call me MJ. Would either of you like a cup of tea? I've discovered I can't actually drink one anymore…' He gestured to several puddles of spilled drink on the tiled floor and a forlorn, smashed cup. 'But it makes me feel better to hold one.'

MJ had bought this cottage some twenty years previously – his country retreat with his beloved Amelia. He saw a red squirrel on the drive the day they came to view and took it as a good omen. He had made thousands of dinners in this kitchen, served countless family buffets and hosted so many happy quiz nights. He could never have imagined that one morning, several days after his own demise, that he'd be sat at this very table listening to Death explain why he was late.

'I really am very sorry,' Graham said as he finished his tale.

'Why?' MJ said, affronted. 'If what you say is true, it sounds like this Sybil woman is the one who owes me an apology - and owes you one too, Max.'

'Sybil's the interpreter and manipulator of destiny,' Graham shrugged. 'If she gave out apologies she'd get nothing else done.'

'Well, I don't mind telling you I feel slightly miffed,' MJ said. 'I don't know how this young lady is so calm. Talk about rough luck.'

Max could feel her cheeks colouring as she remembered Sybil's words in the hospital, the perfectly good life waiting for her, and the purpose she had already served. 'Mm, yes,' she said half-heartedly. 'Miffed.'

Doris flapped back up to her shoulder and perched there, sensing her discomfort.

MJ tapped his hands awkwardly on his cup. 'You know, Max, if I'd known it was you outside my house that night, I...I would have shown my face or something. I feel responsible somehow. Even if it was all predetermined. Does that make sense?'

'It makes sense. I'm sorry I went to your house and not someone else's. If I had, you wouldn't have been stuck here.'

'Well, I've had worse lock-ins,' MJ chuckled. 'And on that subject, I suppose it's time to go, is it?'

'I've seen The Afterward,' Max said. 'The place you go after this. It's weird and beautiful and full of people just like this. You can have a life there – another one.'

'When one door closes another opens, eh?' he said. 'Should I pack a bag?'

'No need,' Graham replied.

The four of them left MJ's cottage and headed back down the drive. The morning mist was beginning to burn off and the familiar smell of bonfires on the air seemed to MJ to be the perfect send-off.

'Make sure the door's shut,' he said as Max stepped out last. 'I don't want the leaves tae blow in.'

'Did you live alone?' Max asked.

'Uh huh,' MJ nodded gently. 'Not always, though. I shared it with my wife. We loved the countryside. Walks in the woods, you know? It's why we moved here.'

He looked back at the house for one last time and wiped his eyes roughly with the back of his hand. 'Amelia is waiting for me on the other side. Such a silly sod. Got in a car wreck two summers ago. Killed instantly, I was told.'

'Oh, gosh, I'm sorry,' Max said.

'You said you'd seen it though, yes? The Afterward?'

'Yes, it's not the harps and cherubs you're probably picturing, but it is something.'

'A turn up for the books, indeed!'

'You're not that old, though. Don't you feel robbed?'

'I suppose that could be my attitude. I was hoping for a lot longer. You know what though? When I saw my own body in that chair, I just felt acceptance. Can't cry over spilt milk!'

'Funny,' Max said. 'That's not how I felt at all.'

'That's because it wasn't your time, lass.'

They reached the end of the driveway and headed towards Graham's van. In the distance, a swirling mass of birds flew across the sky.

'Friends of yours?' MJ asked Doris.

Her little eyes stared skyward: 'Yes. Off to comfort the waiting dead. Still catching up.'

'Hurry up, you guys,' Euryale shouted, leaning her head out the window.

'Just a second,' Max said, jogging off down the road. 'There's something I need to do first.'

'We don't have time for th-' Graham started, but he knew it was futile.

The streaks of rubber on the road told Max she was on the right track. Her little car had already been recovered, but there were fragments of it still strewn in the hedgerow.

She bent down and inspected a piece of wing mirror, her reflection missing. She thought about her car sat in a scrapheap with no one for company – broken, battered, waiting for destruction. Then she thought about her mum, sat in the hospital, holding her only daughter's hand. A lump grew in her throat.

'Hey, what I did I say about you being left alone too long?' Graham said quietly as he approached.

'I miss my life,' Max said. 'I'm so angry at Sybil, at Lennie, at you.'

'I know.'

Aren't you angry too?'

'I think I probably had it coming, Max.'

There was a moment of silence and then both of them smiled.

'Yep,' Max said. 'I think you probably did.'

In the distance they heard Doris squawking and they turned in unison.

'Time to go,' Graham said gently.

They walked back towards the van. Max slid in between MJ and Euryale, while Graham bounced into the driver's seat. Doris was perched on the dashboard, her head wobbling slightly like a plastic novelty ornament.

'This lass has hair snakes,' MJ said excitedly, pointing at Euryale.

'Yes, she does,' Graham said. 'And aren't they beautiful?'

The snakes hissed appreciatively. Graham rubbed his hands together and grinned. 'Now let's get this show on the road.'

'Hey, what are you so happy about?' Max asked.

'Nothing,' he said breezily. 'This is nice, that's all.'

'Not so nice for me, laddie,' said MJ, 'but I think I'm ready.'

'You honestly don't need to worry,' Max said, grabbing his hand.

'I'm glad I'm doing this with you,' he smiled, as the campervan pulled away, leaving Chudleigh behind once and for all.

CHAPTER EIGHTEEN

GIVE UP THE GHOST

The campervan whinnied and lurched down the motorway towards Dover. The weight of carrying not one, but two, unaccounted-for souls threatened to break its engine at any moment.

There would have been a time when the sight of trees and signs crawling by at such a slow pace would have sent Graham into a blind rage, but he was far too busy enjoying himself now.

He pretended for a moment that everyone in the van was on a road trip – perhaps to a festival or a spa. The chaos of the last few days lifted from his shoulders for the briefest of moments and the feeling of weightlessness was delicious.

His phone began to ring in his pocket and the daydream was broken.

'Here we go again,' he sighed.

'Who is it?' Max asked.

Graham drew his phone out of his pocket as if extracting a centipede and showed Max the screen. Azrael's name flashed up in white angular letters.

'You should answer it. Maybe she can help?'

'I'm not stopping, Max. We're still hours away from the ferry.'

'Just pull into the hard shoulder.'

'Hmm, okay.'

Graham brought the van to a stop on a stretch of motorway bordered by a sinewy forest on both sides. Everyone got out and hopped over the barrier. The ground sloped steeply down on the other side and very suddenly the group were stood under a thick canopy of trees.

'Are we there?' MJ asked.

'No, love,' Euryale said soothingly. 'Just a pit stop.'

'Nobody wander too far,' Graham said. 'Doris and Euryale, watch the other two like hawks.'

'I find that a little offensive,' Doris replied.

Graham took a deep breath and raised the phone to his ear.

Doris flapped her wings: 'Okay, kids. Who fancies a nature walk? Let's give Graham some privacy.'

They began slowly walking through the undergrowth. MJ playfully kicked up the golden leaves, his dressing gown cord trailing in the mud. Euryale was softly humming to herself.

'So, what was it like babysitting MJ for three days?' Max asked Doris, as they walked ahead.

'He was okay, you know. He's surprisingly knowledgeable about goth bands of the eighties, so we talked about that, banana bread, supermarket shopping, global warming. You know, the big stuff.'

'For three days?'

'That's nothing. I once had to guard a man in Ealing who insisted I look at his spoon collection. All six thousand of them.'

'I am so sorry.'

Euryale stopped humming: 'Toilet break! Anyone else?' She stared blankly between the bird and the two ghosts. 'Ah, guess not.'

'Don't be long, please,' Doris said as Euryale darted off.

'And then there were three,' Max said.

Standing in the lush green forest watching Doris and Max chatting, MJ had been struck by a wave of nostalgia for his childhood in Glasgow. He remembered running through the park as fast as his legs would carry him and chasing squirrels as high up the trees as he dared to climb.

Suddenly, he heard a rustle in the branches above him. Something small and grey darted with ease from limb to limb of one of the nearby oaks. MJ put his hands in his pockets and pondered. Just one more run through the woods couldn't hurt, could it?

He glanced briefly at Max and Doris, still locked in conversation.

'I'm just looking over here,' he said.

'Stay where I can see you,' Doris shouted after him.

'Just a little leg stretch,' he replied.

He meandered a little further away, following the sound of the animal in the trees.

Doris and Max's voices soon faded as MJ wandered on and soon all he could hear was the birds tweeting and the wind rustling the canopy above him.

The ground underneath, undisturbed by his footsteps, was leaf-strewn and dotted with little insects.

MJ knelt down beside a passing earwig.

'Aren't you just glorious?' he asked it earnestly. The earwig carried on its way – it didn't really want to get involved in anyone's business today.

'Now, where is that squirrel,' he continued. The earwig picked up pace like a person at a bus stop backing away from a drunk. 'Got to be around here somewhere…'

Max and Doris were cackling with laughter when Graham burst through the bushes. He stopped suddenly, a look of concern on his face.

'Where are the other two?'

'Two?' Doris replied.

There was a distant sound of leaves crunching underfoot. Euryale appeared from behind a tree: 'Phew, that feels so much better!'

Her face fell as she looked at the stony faces in front of her: 'What? What's the matter with all of you?'

'MJ,' Max said with a sudden jolt of fear. 'We've lost him.'

'Uh, he was right here!'

'He was.'

Doris flew up higher to try and get a better view. 'He just said he was stretching his legs!'

'He could be anywhere by now,' Graham said exasperatedly.

With cat-like stealth, MJ had stalked the squirrel as it flitted through the canopy. Eventually, it had bobbed down to ground level. He was within metres of it now. It was facing away from him.

'Let me get a good look at your face, laddie,' he said.

Now he could see it properly, it didn't look much like a squirrel at all - its back legs were too long, its body too squat, its tail was entirely stripped of fur.

'Bit wonky aren't you, pal?' MJ said. As the animal turned to look at him he realised with horror that it was a rat. Its whiskers twitched and in an instant it was running towards him. MJ leapt out of the way, shrieking in fright, and the rodent disappeared into the undergrowth.

Under Graham's sweater his cold, unnatural heart was pounding like a bailiff on a locked door. He, Euryale, Max and Doris were making their way through the forest. Occasionally they took turns shouting for MJ, but there was no reply.

Graham turned to glare at Doris and Euryale: 'How could you be so thoughtless?'

'I did my best, Graham,' Doris said. 'I told him not to go too far.'

'Yeah, and I needed the loo. What was I supposed to do?'

'Hold it in!' Graham barked.

Without another word, Doris took off and disappeared from view – a tiny, feathered, angry line in the sky.

Graham sighed and threw his hands up in the air. 'Come on,' he gestured to Max and Euryale. 'We have to find him before he…'

Max butted in: 'Endlessly drifts on the winds of time as a confused and frightened wisp of former human consciousness? Yeah, I know.'

The wind toyed with MJ's hair. The trees looked alien and identical. He no longer knew the way forward.

'Ah,' he said, looking around for any sign of the way back. 'Where's the satnav when you need it?'

He heard a stream babbling in the distance and decided a landmark would be the most logical place to sit and wait for a fresh thought to materialise. He made his way further into the woods and slowly dusk began folding its arms around him.

Max wasn't sure how much time had passed, but it had to have been a little while because the sun had set and Graham was beginning to sound slightly delirious.

'I hope nothing's happened to him,' Euryale said.

'How did he just disappear?' Graham squeaked as they fought their way through thick forest. 'You said you were only chatting for a little bit!'

'We were waiting for you, remember? What did Azrael want?'

'I don't want to get into it now.'

'Graham, you have to talk to me about this stuff.'

The wood was filled with unfamiliar sounds and only the outline of the trees, in front of the plum sky, was visible. There was the sound of a stream now, trickling somewhere ahead. Still they strode on blindly - branches scratching their faces and roots threatening to trip them every other step.

'I don't. It doesn't matter.'

'What did she say, Graham?'

'She said the board were coming for me and to turn myself in. Then she sent a text.'

Graham passed his phone forward to Max and she stopped to read the illuminated words: 'They've traced the call. Run if you can.'

Max turned the phone back to shine it in Graham's face.

'How long do you have?' she asked and then she screamed. The glow had revealed a crouched figure just a few metres away. It was MJ.

The light passed through him and illuminated the stream – like a single tear of mercury in a sea of black velvet.

'Oh, thank goodness,' Max said. 'MJ! MJ?'

'No, wait,' Graham said leaning to grab her, but she had already stepped forward.

'We were so worried,' she said. 'We've been going around these woods for ages.'

There were only the sounds of the forest and then rustling fabric as MJ turned to face them. Max's smile dropped as she realised there was no saving him now - his whole body looked like smoke held in a glass bottle.

'Amelia, is that you?' MJ said. 'Can you help me? I think I'm waiting for someone.'

'MJ, it's us. *We're* who you were waiting for.' Max could feel a lump rising in her throat, but she forced it down.

'Oh! Oh yes of course, how silly of me, yes. Well, let's go then,' he smiled back.

'It's okay,' she said. 'No harm done!'
Graham approached slowly and gently moved Max to the side. Euryale held her hand

'I'm so sorry,' Graham said to MJ. 'I took my eye off the ball and you paid the price. You didn't deserve it. You're not alone.'

'Surely he remembers something,' Max protested. 'It's not too late! I've come back from this.'

She turned back to MJ, 'Come on, now,' she said gently. 'Let's get you to the ferry.'

But his brow was furrowed in confusion. 'Can you help me, dear?' he said. 'I think I'm waiting for someone.'

Graham, Max and Euryale stood silently in the dark.

'Hello,' Max said, voice cracking. 'I'm Max.'

'Hello, lass. Such a lovely name,' MJ said smiling, his voice getting fainter by the second. He stretched out a hand to shake, but before Max could touch his fingers they had drifted away.

'Have you seen my Amelia?' he sighed.

Max let out a sob as tears streamed down her face. 'Is there nothing we can do?' she said.

Graham shook his head. Euryale put her hand to her mouth to stop herself from crying.

Only MJ's face remained now. His kind, confused eyes held with Max's as he faded slowly into the night like breath in winter air.

CHAPTER NINETEEN

THE GREAT EQUALISER

Graham and Max sat quietly in the van now parked at a motorway service station. They watched the dark road running left to right in front of them. Brilliant headlamps appeared over the brow of the hill, streaked like shooting stars and disappeared round a bend with a red spark of rear lights.

One of them was Euryale, catching a lift after a tearful goodbye.

Max could feel her eyes burning from the crying, her whole face felt swollen. Graham wiped his face roughly with his hand, his mouth turned down in sorrow.

'I'll make sure they get you back to the hospital,' he sighed. 'You'll be okay.'

'Will you?'

'I don't know what happens to a retired psychopomp. Perhaps I'll disappear like MJ.'

'No,' Max said, holding his hand. 'Not another one, not tonight.'

He squeezed her fingers and put a weak smile on his face. With the other hand he turned on the van radio.

Max rubbed her nose with her sleeve: 'You mean we could have been listening to music this whole time?'

'The last time I turned this radio on was 1993, so consider yourself honoured!'

Out of the static came a tune familiar to both their ears, but it meant something more to Max.

'Sybil's close,' she said, her voice lowering.

'How do you know?'

'Because this is the song that was playing when my car crashed.'

They both hummed along mutedly to Dolly Parton as, sure enough, a pair of lights peeled off the road and pulled into the car park. A grey estate car rolled almost silently to a stop next to the campervan.

'Time to face the music,' Graham said and they both got out of the van and stood in the cold night air. Three more cars rolled up and parked a short distance away – one black, one red, one white. The windscreens were too dark to see through, but Graham knew that Lennie, Flannery and his eldest sister Euna were watching proceedings intently. He could not be entirely sure if they were there to feed him to the lions or defend him from them. They were that kind of family.

There was a loud click as the grey car's passenger door opened and out shambled five figures, draped in a kind of black clinging fog that obscured their form. One figure was entirely discernible though – her shocking pink hair instantly gave her away.

'You!' Max said, her anger propelling her forwards before Graham pulled her back. 'I suppose you're going to tell us MJ died for a reason too? Was he special, Sybil? Was he perfectly designed to teach a lesson?'

'You know it's pointless to be angry with me, dear. I'm afraid Mr Mallory was doomed from the moment of his birth. I gave him three days post-mortem, I think that's rather generous!'

'More generous than eternity?'

'They're pretty much the same thing, petal, really when it all comes down to it.'

'What about his wife, huh? Waiting in The Afterward?'

'Oh, don't be so naive, girl!' Sybil said as she rolled her eyes. 'She's been shacked up with a dead stockbroker for a year. 'Till death do us part, remember"

Max glared at her.

'Pout at me all you want, but my job is not to be the most popular girl at prom!' Sybil said, rolling up her sleeves. 'My job is to keep the cosmos in order so down is down and up is up. You cannot conceive of the many timelines in my head, the chess pieces I have to move to keep everything going as it was ordained. It is exhausting!'

Graham stepped forward: 'Let's get this over with shall we, Sybil? One more of your monologues and my preordained path will be to plug my ears with the first soft thing I find. Get the chicken in here and put me in prison or whatever it is you do with beings like me.'

Sybil smiled and ran a hand through her wispy hair. 'Graham, my dear, your fortunes have improved considerably since the last time we spoke.'

'What does that mean?'

'It means the job is yours, if you want it.'

Graham stared at the group of amorphous shadow figures standing motionless in front of him.

'I don't understand,' he said, clutching his head in exasperation. 'I nearly got arrested. Now you tell me I can just crack on? After I failed a defenceless soul in the most terrible way?'

Sybil stood perfectly still and watched Graham with a smug smile slowly creeping across her face. The penny she had pushed towards the edge of the precipice in her Florida bungalow was about to drop.

'I had to feel it,' Graham said, numbly. 'I couldn't just *want* the job back. You wanted me to grieve a loss too for good measure.'

'The lesson wasn't over,' Sybil said. 'How can you ever truly value anything if you've never lost it? Think yourself jolly lucky. It should have been your little friend, but after your performance at Flannery's we came to another arrangement.'

Max and Graham were silent for a moment, holding hands in the freezing car park.

Graham felt an anger washing over him so large it could engulf his very being. The ground beneath him seemed to flow upwards like a river of molasses seeping over his shoes, up his legs and body and finally covering his head. Max stumbled backwards, watching as Graham grew taller. The black spreading outwards until the man she had known for these brief few days was no longer recognisable. In his place stood Death – skeletal, towering, cold, and ruthless.

For the first time since their meeting, Max understood the true nature of the being she had been travelling with. The ancient power of him seemed to seep out of his flowing robes and permeate the air around him like static electricity. He was utterly terrifying.

Sybil had not moved from her spot, but she stared up with a touch of awe.

'You dare manipulate me?' he boomed at Sybil, his bleached teeth clattering in his empty skull. 'You dare put me at the mercy of the winds of change? I am not a mortal plaything for you to toss about, Sybil!'

One of Sybil's hands began to quiver and she steadied it quickly with the other, gripping hard. 'You're welcome,' she said.

'You're going to take her back to her body first,' Death said, pointing a bony finger at Max. 'I want to watch her go back and you will give me your word that you aren't going to kill her as soon as you're able.'

'Yes please,' Max squeaked.

'And I want Simon to go back to being a happy little chicken on some farm somewhere,' he continued. 'An actual farm, not the pretend farm that everyone's pet goes to, got it? And more than that, I want a say in this whole business. You wanted me to care? Well now I do and I'm not going to be your minion. I want control. I want delegation. I want... an office!'

Sybil looked at the shadowy figures and they turned to each other and silently nodded in approval.

'It's a deal.'

The first bloom of sunrise was just illuminating the sky when Max, Sybil, and Graham, now back to his usual proportions, walked into the hospital room for the last time.

Max's mum was sitting awkwardly in a chair with her head slumped against the bed. Her hand was still holding Max's.

'Oof, she's going to regret that when she wakes up,' Graham chuckled.

'I think she'll possibly have bigger fish to fry,' Max replied. 'So, how does this work then? Do I lie on top of myself or say some magic words or what?'

Sybil stepped forward and put her hands on Max's shoulders: 'You've nearly done it once before, remember? When you're ready, close your eyes and focus on your body's breathing. Touch your own hand if it helps.'

Max turned to look at Graham. She opened her mouth to speak, but Graham interrupted her.

'No goodbyes,' he said. 'Fortunately for me, I know we'll meet again one day. Thank you though... for everything.'

Max couldn't help throwing her arms around him and they held each other tightly for a second.

'Thank you,' Max said, then turned to face her own body and closed her eyes. She felt a stillness wash over her as her mind drifted through her journey since the car crash. She felt herself reach out an arm to touch her own hand and then hold it tightly. Minutes seemed to tick by with nothing happening.

'Umm, guys? I don't think it's working.'

The words felt stiff in her mouth, her speech slurred and incomprehensible. She opened her eyes slowly and realised the hand she thought she was squeezing was her mother's and she was staring with utmost concern at Max's face.

Graham and Sybil watched on from the doorway as mother and daughter embraced and held each other tightly, both with tears running down their faces.

'Mortals, eh?' Graham said, wiping a solitary tear from his own tired eyes.

'Let's go see that office those tears have bought you,' Sybil replied and both of them disappeared around the corner.

CHAPTER TWENTY

RIP

A gentle breeze blew through the willow tree at the end of Max's garden as she sank her toes in the soft grass. The warmth of the sun on her face against her closed, wrinkled eyes made her smile.

The cold gusts of spring were just beginning to turn to the warmth of summer. Soon the sweet smells of roses and sun cream would fill the air. But she knew in her heart she wouldn't experience it this year.

She had begun to feel stretched thinner and thinner, like inflated bubblegum ready to pop. Pain was a constant companion now and her joints protested with every movement.

A dark shadow passed over her eyelids and she opened them to glare at the impudent cloud responsible for blocking her light. But instead, there stood a familiar figure gazing down at her, a giant scythe in his hand.

Graham smiled warmly. 'Hello there, old woman!'

'Well, I am pleased to see you,' Max said.

'Don't hear that very often,' Graham scoffed. 'Bet you don't get that very often?'

'It's good you're here actually. I was getting a bit chilly truth be told.'

'Hmm,' Graham replied.

'Hmm? What does that mean?'

'I don't think you're quite where you imagine you are, Max.'

She looked around and realised he was right. Where the willow tree had been, there now stood a hat stand. The beautiful blue sky had become regimented grid of polystyrene tiles. The warm grass was the soft bed blankets covering her feet.

She heard a soft whimper and knew she and Graham were not alone. There were three middle-aged people, all with sombre, down-turned mouths at her bedside. A man on the far left of Max grabbed her hand and she was comforted by it even though she could no longer feel his touch.

'Goodbye, Mum,' he croaked. A woman next to him silently put her hand on his shoulder and squeezed. The younger man next to her did the same.

'Oh my,' Max said. 'They must have given me a stupendous amount of drugs.'

'Rock and roll!' Graham grinned.

Max moved herself out of bed with a sense of ease she had not felt in years and looked at her children, their heads bowed in the presence of her frail frame under the covers. Her eyes began brimming with tears.

'I'm so proud of them,' she whispered to Graham. 'When did they get so old? When did I?' She touched her silver hair with a papery hand adorned with a golden serpent ring.

'I've been waiting a while for you,' Graham said.

'Oh charming! Breathing down my neck, were you?'

'Well there was that one time before Christmas when you decided to cross the road without looking...'

'Yes, that was a bit close.'

'Or last May when you forgot to change the batteries in your smoke alarm and fell asleep with dinner in the oven...'

'Oh!' she scolded. 'My son already gave me a right earful over that one.'

'Smart kid. You're a menace to society!'

Max watched her children hold each other and felt a surge of love and pride. 'I was so prepared for you,' she sighed. 'But I wasn't prepared to say goodbye.... Let's blow this joint, eh? If I look at the faces of these poor kids another minute, you'll have to drag me out of here.'

She kissed each one of her children on the forehead. 'Goodbye, loveys, but not forever.'

It would be several years before all three of them discussed it together, but the children would come to realise that in that moment they had all felt the same surge of comfort and affection that let them know their mother had truly left the room.

Graham and Max walked in silence to the elevator. The heat and smell of disinfectant reminded them both of their time in Swindon so very many years ago.

'I always told the kids I would meet death as an old friend,' Max chuckled as the lift doors slowly closed after them. 'I think they thought I was talking in metaphors.'

'Or bollocks,' Graham laughed.

'Exactly. I do like the scythe, by the way.'

'Oh, thanks!' Graham said, adjusting the top of the massive blade to stop it scraping the lift ceiling. 'After I left you I had a little... rebrand. Time to go back to the old ways, you know? Stick to the classics!'

'Well, it certainly adds a bit of gravitas.'

The two stood in silence for a moment with only the mechanical hum of the lift for company.

'Ah, come here,' Graham motioned for her to hug him and they folded their arms around each other and squeezed hard.

'I can't believe it's really time to go,' Max said, turning her face up to Graham and smiling.

'That cottage you asked for is waiting for you,' Graham said as he motioned her into the entrance hall. 'But actually, given our history, the board have granted me special permissions not to take you to the port straight away.'

'Really? How interesting,' grinned Max.

'I don't suppose you fancy a little drive before eternity?'

'What about all the other souls?'

'I've got a bit of help these days. I get four weeks of paid leave, you know!'

As the pair wandered out into the cold, evening air, Max spotted the green campervan parked up in front of her. It seemed shinier and fresher than it ever had.

'Looks like you're not the only one who had a rebrand,' Max gasped as the van engine rumbled back in approval.

Graham broke into a little half-run of excitement as he held the passenger door open for Max and she climbed in with a sigh of happy familiarity.

Graham hopped in beside her and placed both his hands on the wheel. He turned to look at her and grinned. 'I need you to help me end the world.'

THE END

About the Author

Rachael Atkins was born in Dorset a long time ago. She devoured books whole as a child and wrote her first comic book aged seven.

Grim Harvest is Rachael's debut novel. She began writing it in university and totally meant to leave it unfinished for fifteen years. Honestly.

Since leaving this book languishing on her computer she has become a journalist, an award-winning radio presenter, a voiceover artist, and a children's author.

She lives in a pink house in Devon with her husband and daughter.

Printed in Great Britain
by Amazon